CRIME

Ferdinand von Schirach

Translated from the German by
Carol Brown Janeway

Chatto & Windus
LONDON

Published by Chatto & Windus 2011

2 4 6 8 10 9 7 5 3 1

Copyright © Piper Verlag GmbH, München 2009
Translation copyright © Carol Brown Janeway 2011

Originally published in German as *Verbrechen* in 2009 by Piper Verlag GmbH

Ferdinand von Schirach has asserted his right under the Copyright, Designs and Patents Act 1988 to be identified as the author of this work

First published in Great Britain in 2011 by
Chatto & Windus
Random House, 20 Vauxhall Bridge Road,
London SW1V 2SA
www.rbooks.co.uk

Addresses for companies within The Random House Group Limited can be
found at: www.randomhouse.co.uk/offices.htm

The Random House Group Limited Reg. No. 954009

A CIP catalogue record for this book
is available from the British Library

ISBN 9780701185473

The Random House Group Limited supports The Forest Stewardship
Council (FSC), the leading international forest certification organisation.
All our titles that are printed on Greenpeace approved FSC certified paper
carry the FSC logo. Our paper procurement policy can be found at
www.rbooks.co.uk/environment

CONTENTS

The reality we can put into words is never reality itself.

Werner K. Heisenberg

Preface
Guilt

Jim Jarmusch once said he'd rather make a movie about a man walking his dog than about the Emperor of China. I feel the same way. I write about criminal cases, I've appeared for the defence in more than seven hundred of them. But actually my subject is human beings—their failings, their guilt, and their capacity to behave magnificently.

I had an uncle who was the presiding judge over a court that heard trials by jury. These are the courts that handle capital offences: murder and manslaughter. He told us stories from these cases that we could understand, even as children. They always began with him saying: 'Most things are complicated, and guilt always presents a bit of a problem.'

He was right. We chase after things, but they're faster than we are, and in the end we can never catch up. I tell the stories of people I've defended. They were murderers, drug dealers, bank robbers and prostitutes. They all had their stories, and they weren't so different from us. All our lives we dance on a thin layer of ice; it's very cold underneath, and death is quick. The ice won't bear the weight of some people and they fall through. That's the moment that interests me. If we're lucky, it never happens to us and we keep dancing. If we're lucky.

My uncle was in the navy during the war, and lost his left arm and right hand to a grenade. Despite this, he didn't give up for a long time. People say he was a good judge, humane, an upright man with a sense of justice. He loved going hunting, and had a little private blind. His gun was custom-made for him and he could use it with one hand. One day he went into the woods, put the double-barrelled shotgun in his mouth, and pulled the trigger. He was wearing a black roll-neck sweater; he'd hung his jacket on a branch. His head exploded. I saw the photos a long time later. He left a letter for his best friend, in which he wrote that he'd simply had enough. The letter began with the words 'Most things are complicated, and guilt always presents a bit of a problem.' I still miss him. Every day.

This book is about people like him, and their stories.

FvS

Fähner

Friedhelm Fähner had spent his whole working life as a GP in Rottweil, 2,800 patients with medical insurance processed every year, doctor's office on the main street, chairman of the Egyptian Cultural Association, member of the Lions Club, no criminal offences, nor even minor infringements. Besides his house, he owned two rental properties, a three-year-old E-Class Mercedes with leather upholstery and air conditioning, approximately 750,000 euros in bonds, and a capital sum life insurance policy. Fähner had no children. His only living relative was his sister, six years younger, who lived in Stuttgart with her husband and two sons. Fähner's life wasn't anything that gave rise to stories.

Until the thing with Ingrid.

Fähner was twenty-four when he met Ingrid at the party to celebrate his father's sixtieth birthday. His father had been a doctor in Rottweil, too.

As a town, Rottweil is bourgeois to the core. Any non-inhabitant will be vouchsafed the information, willy-nilly, that the town was founded a thousand years ago and is the oldest in Baden-Württemberg. And indeed you come across medieval oriel windows and pretty antique tavern signs from the sixteenth century. The Fähners had lived here forever. They belonged to the so-called first families of the town, known for their roles as doctors, judges and apothecaries.

Friedhelm Fähner looked a little like the young John F. Kennedy. He had a friendly face, people took him to be carefree, and things always panned out for him. You had to look more closely to detect a certain sadness, some ancient dark shadow in his expression, not so uncommon in this land between the Black Forest and the mountains of Swabia.

Ingrid's parents, who were pharmacists in Rottweil, took their daughter with them to the party. She was three years older than Fähner, a sturdy, big-breasted provincial beauty. Eyes of a watery blue, black hair, pale skin—she knew the effect she had on people. Her voice, high-pitched and strangely metallic, grated on Fähner. It was only when she spoke softly that her sentences found a melody of their own.

She had failed to complete high school and was working as a waitress. 'Temporarily,' she said to Fähner. He didn't care. In another area, and one that interested him much more, she was way ahead of him. Fähner had had only two sexual encounters with women; they had been more unsettling than anything. He promptly fell in love with Ingrid.

Two days after the birthday party, she seduced him at the end of a picnic. They lay in a hikers' shelter and Ingrid did her stuff well. Fähner was so overwhelmed that only a week later he asked her to marry him. She accepted without hesitation: Fähner was what you'd call a good catch, he was studying medicine in Munich, he was attractive and caring, and he would soon be taking his first exams. But what attracted her most was his seriousness. She couldn't put it into words, but she said to her girlfriend that Fähner would never walk out on her. Four months later, she moved in with him.

The honeymoon was a trip to Cairo, his choice. When people later asked him about Egypt, he said it floated free of the earth, even when he knew that nobody would understand what he meant. Over there he was the young Parsifal, his purity that of a holy fool, and he was happy. It was the last time in his life.

The evening before they flew back, they were lying in their hotel room. The windows were open; it was still too hot, the air a solid mass in the little room. It was a cheap hotel, it smelled of rotten fruit, and they could hear the sounds of the street below. Despite the heat, they had made love. Fähner lay on his back, watching the rotations of the ceiling fan, as Ingrid smoked a cigarette. She turned on her side, propped her head on one hand, and looked at him. He smiled. There was a long silence.

Then she began to tell her story. She told Fähner about the men who'd come before him, about disappointments and mistakes, but most of all about the French lieutenant who had gotten her pregnant, and the abortion that had almost killed her. She wept. Shocked, he took her in his arms. He felt her heart beating against his chest and was undone. She has entrusted herself to me, he thought.

'You must swear to look after me. You can't ever leave me.' Ingrid's voice trembled.

He was moved. He wanted to calm her. He said he'd already sworn to do this at the wedding ceremony in church. He was happy with her. He wanted—

She interrupted him brusquely, her voice rising and taking on its unmodulated metallic sheen. 'Swear.'

And suddenly he understood. This was no conversation between lovers, under the fan in Cairo, with the pyramids and the stifling heat of their hotel room—all these clichés vanished in an instant. He pushed her away a little so that he could see her eyes. Then he said it. He said it slowly, and he knew what he was saying. 'I swear.'

He pulled her close once more and kissed her face. They made love again. But this time it was different. She sat on top of him, took whatever she wanted. They were deadly serious, strangers to each other, and each of them was wholly alone. Afterward, he lay awake for a long time, staring at the ceiling. There had been a power cut and the fan had stopped revolving.

Naturally, Fähner passed his exams with distinction, completed his doctorate, and landed his first job in the Rott-weil District Hospital. They found an apartment, three rooms, bath, view of the edge of the forest.

When his things in Munich were being packed up, she threw out his record collection. He didn't realise this until they were moving into the new apartment. She said she couldn't stand them—he'd listened to them with other women. Fähner was furious. They barely spoke to each other for two days.

Fähner liked Bauhaus clarity. She decorated the apartment in oak and pine, hung curtains at the windows, and bought brightly coloured bed linens. He even accepted the embroidered coasters and the pewter tankards; he didn't want to put her down.

A few weeks later, Ingrid told him she was bothered by the way he held his knife and fork. To begin with, he laughed and thought she was being childish. She reproached him with it again the next day, and then the days after that. And because she meant it, he took to holding his knife differently.

Ingrid pretended that he didn't take out the garbage. He persuaded himself that these were merely teething troubles in their relationship. But soon she was accusing him of coming home too late because he'd been flirting with other women.

The reproaches became unending, until he was hearing them daily: he was disorganised. He dirtied his shirts. He crumpled the newspaper. He smelled bad. He thought only of himself. He talked nonsense. He was cheating on her. Fähner barely defended himself anymore.

After a few years, the insults began. Relatively measured at first, they then gained in intensity. He was a pig. He was torturing her. He was an idiot. Then came the scatological rants and the screaming. He gave up. He would get out of bed during the night and read science fiction. He went jogging for an hour every day, as he had done when he was a student. They had long since given up sex. He received approaches from other women, but he never had an affair. When he was thirty-five, he took over his father's practice; when he was forty, he had turned grey. Fähner was tired.

—

When Fähner was forty-eight, his father died; when he was fifty, it was his mother's turn. He used his inheritance to buy a half-timbered house on the outskirts of town. The house came with a small park, a wilderness of shrubs, forty apple trees, twelve chestnut trees and a pond. The garden became Fähner's salvation. He ordered books, subscribed to specialist journals, and read everything he could lay his hands on about shrubs, ponds and trees. He bought the best tools, informed himself about watering systems, and learned everything there was to learn with his customary systematic thoroughness. The garden blossomed, and the plantings became so famous in the neighbourhood that Fähner saw people here and there among the apple trees taking photographs of them.

During the week, he spent long hours at his practice. Fähner was a painstaking and empathetic doctor. His patients thought highly of him; his diagnoses set the standard in Rottweil. He left the house before Ingrid woke up and didn't return until after nine in the evening. He accepted the nightly barrage of reproaches at dinner in silence. Sentence by unvarnished sentence, Ingrid's metallic voice laid down animosity after animosity like railroad tracks. She had grown fat and her pale skin had turned pink with the years. Her neck had thickened and begun to wobble, and she had developed a fold of skin at her throat that swayed in time to her outbursts. She became short of breath and had high blood pressure. Fähner got thinner and thinner. One evening when he blurted out that Ingrid might perhaps seek help from a psychiatrist who was a friend, she threw a frying pan at him and screamed that he was an ungrateful pig.

The night before Fähner's sixtieth birthday, he lay awake. He had pulled out the faded photo from Egypt: Ingrid and himself in front of the Pyramid of Cheops, with a background of camels, scenic Bedouins and sand. When she threw out their wedding albums, he had fished the picture back up out of the garbage. Since then, it had found a safe hiding place deep in the back of his closet.

In the course of this night, Fähner was forced to realise that he would remain an eternal prisoner until the end of his life. He had given his word in Cairo. And now, in the bad times, was when he had to keep it; there was no such thing as giving your word for the good times only. The photo swam before his eyes. He took off his clothes and stood naked in front of the bathroom mirror. He looked at himself for a long time. Then he sat on the rim of the bathtub. For the first time in his adult life, he cried.

Fähner was working in his garden. He was seventy-two now; he'd sold his practice four years before. As always, he had gotten up at six o'clock. He had left the guest room—in which he'd been living for years—very quietly. Ingrid was still asleep. It was a glowing September morning. The early mist had burned off and the air was clear and cold. Fähner was using a hoe to weed the ground between the autumn perennials. It was an activity both demanding and monotonous. Fähner was content. He looked forward to the coffee he would be drinking at nine-thirty, something he always did when he took his break. Fähner also thought about the delphiniums he'd planted early in the year. They would blossom for a third time late in the fall.

Suddenly, Ingrid yanked open the door to the terrace. She yelled that he'd forgotten once again to close the windows in the guest room, said he was a total idiot. Her voice cracked— the sound of pure metal fracturing.

Later on, Fähner would be unable to describe exactly what went through his mind at that moment. That something deep inside him had begun to glow with a hard, clear light. That everything had taken on a supernatural clarity under this light. That it was white-hot.

He asked Ingrid to go down to the cellar, and led the way down the outside stairs himself. Ingrid was pouting as she entered the basement space where he kept his garden tools hanging on the wall, organised by size and function, or standing freshly cleaned in tin and plastic buckets. They were beautiful implements, which he had assembled over the years. As she opened the door, Fähner, without saying a word, lifted the tree axe off the wall. It had been hand-forged in Sweden, was perfectly greased and rust-free. Ingrid fell silent. He was still wearing his coarse gardening gloves. Ingrid stared at the axe. She didn't try to dodge. The first blow that cleaved her skull was enough to kill her. The axe, covered in bone fragments, drove itself deeper into her brain, and the blade split open her face. She was dead before she even hit the ground.

Fähner had to struggle to lever the axe out of her skull, setting his foot against her neck. With two massive blows, he severed the head from the torso. The forensic expert later identified seventeen further blows Fähner had required to separate the arms and the legs.

Fähner gasped for breath. He sat down on the little wooden stool that he'd always used when planting things out. Its legs were standing in blood. Fähner felt hungry. At some point, he stood up, undressed himself next to the corpse at the garden sink and washed the blood out of his hair and off his face. He locked the cellar and climbed the indoor stairs to the living quarters. Once up there, he got dressed again, dialled the police emergency number, gave his name and address, and said, word for word, 'I've made Ingrid small. Come at once.' The call was recorded. Without waiting for a response, he hung up. There had been no agitation in his voice.

A few minutes after the call, the police pulled up in front of Fähner's house without sirens or blue flashing lights. One of them had been in the force for twenty-nine years and his entire family were patients of Dr Fähner. Fähner was standing outside the garden gate and handed him the key. He said she was in the cellar. The policeman knew it would be better not to ask any questions—Fähner was wearing a suit but no shoes or socks. He was very calm.

The trial lasted four days. The presiding judge was an experienced jurist. He knew Fähner, over whom he had to pass judgment. And he knew Ingrid. If he hadn't known her sufficiently well, the witnesses provided the necessary information. Every one of them expressed sympathy for Fähner; every one of them was on his side. The mailman said Fähner was 'a saint' and 'how he'd put up with her' was 'a miracle'. The psychiatrist certified that Fähner had suffered an 'emotional block', although he was not free of criminal responsibility.

The prosecutor asked for eight years. He took his time; he described the sequence of events and went wading through the blood in the cellar. Then he said that Fähner had had other options; he could have gotten a divorce.

The prosecutor was wrong; a divorce was precisely what had not been an option for Fähner. The most recent reform of the code of criminal procedure has dismissed the oath as an obligatory component of any sworn testimony in a criminal case. We ceased believing in it a long time ago. When a witness lies, he lies—no judge seriously thinks an oath would make him do otherwise, and oaths appear to leave our contemporaries indifferent. But, and this 'but' encompasses whole universes, Fähner was not what you'd consider one of our contemporaries. His promise, once given, was inviolable. Promises had bound him all his life; indeed, he was their prisoner. Fähner could not have freed himself; to do so would have amounted to betrayal. The eruption of violence represented the bursting of the pressurised container in which he had been confined his whole life by his oath once given.

Fähner's sister, who had asked me to take on her brother's defence, sat in the public gallery. She wept. His former head nurse held her hand. Fähner had become even thinner in prison. He sat motionless on the dark wooden defendant's bench.

With regard to the practicalities of the case, there was nothing to defend. It was, rather, a problem of judicial philosophy: what is the meaning of punishment? Why do we punish? I used my summation to try to establish this. There is a whole host of theories. Punishment should be a deterrent. Punishment should protect us. Punishment should make the perpetrator avoid any such act in the future. Punishment should counterbalance injustice. Our laws are a composite of these theories, but none of them fitted this case exactly. Fähner would not kill again. The injustice of his act was self-evident but difficult to measure. And who wanted to exercise revenge? It was a long summation. I told his story. I wanted people to understand that Fähner had reached the end. I spoke until I felt I had gotten through to the court. When one of the jurors nodded, I sat down again.

Fähner had the last word. At the end of a trial the court hears the defendant, and the judges have to weigh what he says in their deliberations. He bowed and his hands were clasped one inside the other. He hadn't had to learn his speech by heart; it was the encapsulation of his entire life.

'I loved my wife, and in the end I killed her. I still love her, that is what I promised her, and she is still my wife. This will be true for the rest of my life. I broke my promise. I have to live with my guilt.'

Fähner sat down again in silence and stared at the floor. The courtroom was absolutely silent; even the presiding judge seemed to be filled with trepidation. Then he said that the members of the court would withdraw to begin their deliberations and that the verdict would be pronounced the next day.

That evening, I visited Fähner in jail one more time. There wasn't much left to say. He had brought a crumpled envelope with him, out of which he extracted the photograph from their honeymoon, and ran his thumb over Ingrid's face. The coating on the photo had long since worn away; her face was almost a blank.

Fähner was sentenced to three years, the arrest warrant was withdrawn, and he was freed from custody. He would be permitted to serve his sentence on daytime release. Daytime release means that the person under sentence must spend nights in jail but is allowed out during the day. The condition is that he must pursue a trade or hold a job. It wasn't easy to find a new trade for a seventy-two-year-old. Eventually, it was his sister who did this: Fähner worked as a greengrocer—he sold the apples from his garden.

Four months later, a little crate arrived at my chambers, containing ten red apples. There was an envelope enclosed and in the envelope was a single sheet of paper: 'The apples are good this year. Fähner.'

Tanata's Tea Bowl

They were at one of those free-for-all student parties in Berlin. These were always good for a couple of girls ready to get it on with boys from Kreuzberg and Neukölln, just because they were different. Perhaps what attracted the girls was an inherent vulnerability. This time, Samir seemed to have struck it lucky again: she had blue eyes and laughed a lot.

Suddenly, her boyfriend appeared. He said Samir should get lost or they'd take it out onto the street. Samir didn't understand what 'take it out' meant, but he understood the aggression. They were hustled outside. One of the older students told Samir the guy was an amateur boxer and university champion. Samir said, 'So fucking what?' He was just seventeen, but he was a veteran of more than 150 street fights, and there were very few things he was afraid of— fights were not among them.

The boxer was heavily muscled, a head taller, and a good deal more solidly built than Samir. And he was grinning like an idiot. A circle formed around the two of them, and while the boxer was still taking off his jacket, Samir landed the toe of one shoe right in his balls. His shoe caps were steel-lined; the boxer emitted a gurgle and almost doubled up with pain. Samir seized his head by the hair, yanked it straight down, and simultaneously rammed his right knee into the boxer's face. Although there was a lot of noise on the street, you could hear the boxer's jaw snap. He lay bleeding on the asphalt, one hand over his crotch, the other over his face. Samir took a two-step run-up; the kick broke two of the boxer's ribs.

Samir felt he'd played fair. He hadn't kicked the guy's face and, most important, he hadn't used his knife. It had all been very easy; he wasn't even out of breath. He got angry because the blonde wouldn't take off with him, just cried and fussed over the man on the ground. 'Fucking whore,' he said, and went home.

The judge in juvenile court sentenced Samir to two weeks' custody and obligatory participation in an antiviolence seminar. Samir tried to explain to the social workers in the juvenile detention centre that the conviction was wrong. The boxer had started it; it was just that he himself had been quicker. That sort of thing wasn't a game. You could play football, but nobody played at boxing. The judge had simply failed to understand the rules.

Özcan collected Samir from jail when the two weeks were up. Özcan was Samir's best friend. He was eighteen, a tall, slow-moving boy with a doughy face. He'd had his first girlfriend when he was twelve, and had videoed everything they got up to with his mobile phone, which earned him his place as top dog forever. Özcan's penis was ridiculously large, and whenever he was in a public lavatory he positioned himself so that everyone else could see. The one thing he was determined to do was to get to New York. He'd never been there and he spoke no English, but he was obsessed with the city. You never saw him without his dark blue cap with NY on it. He wanted to run a nightclub in Manhattan that had a restaurant and go-go dancers. Or whatever. He couldn't explain why it had to be New York, specifically, but he didn't waste any time thinking about it. Özcan's father had spent his whole life in a factory that made lightbulbs; he had arrived from Turkey with nothing but a single suitcase. His son was his hope. He didn't understand the New York thing at all.

Özcan told Samir he'd met someone who had a plan. His name was Manólis. It was a good plan, but Manólis 'was nuts'.

Manólis came from a Greek family that owned a string of restaurants and internet cafes in Kreuzberg and Neukölln. He had passed his high school diploma and started to study history, with a sideline in drugs. A few years ago, something had gone wrong. The suitcase that was supposed to have cocaine in it turned out to be full of paper and sand. The buyer fired at Manólis when he tried to flee in his car with the money. The buyer was a lousy shot, and eight of the nine bullets missed. The ninth penetrated the back of Manólis's skull and lodged there. It was still in Manólis's head when he collided with a squad car. It wasn't till he was in the hospital that the doctors discovered it, and since then Manólis had had a problem. After the operation, he announced to his family

17

that he was now a Finn, celebrated the sixth of December every year as Finland's national holiday, and tried in vain to learn the language. Besides this, he had moments when he was completely out of it, so perhaps his plan wasn't really a fully worked-out one.

But Samir still thought it had some potential. Manólis's sister had a friend who worked as a cleaning lady in a villa in Dahlem. She was in urgent need of money, so all she wanted from Manólis was a small cut if he broke into the house. She knew the alarm code and the one for the electronic lock, she knew where the safe was, and, most important, she knew that the owner would soon be away from Berlin for four days. Samir and Özcan agreed immediately.

The night before the break-in, Samir slept badly, dreaming about Manólis and Finland. When he woke, it was two in the afternoon. He said, 'Fuck judges,' and chased his girlfriend out of bed. At four o'clock, he had to be at the antiviolence class.

Özcan picked up the others at 2:00 a.m. Manólis had fallen asleep, and Samir and Özcan had to wait outside his door for twenty minutes. It was cold; the car windows misted up. They got lost and screamed at one another. It was almost three o'clock when they reached Dahlem. They pulled the black ski masks on in the car; they were too big, they slipped down and scratched, and they were sweating underneath them. Özcan got a tangle of wool fluff in his mouth and spat it out onto the dashboard. They put on latex gloves and ran across the gravel path to the entrance of the villa.

Manólis punched in the code on the lock pad. The door opened with a click. The alarm was in the entryway. After Manólis had fed in a combination of numbers, the little lights switched from red to green. Özcan had to laugh. 'Özcan's Eleven,' he said out loud. He loved movies. The tension eased. It had never been so easy. The front door clicked shut; they were standing in darkness.

They couldn't find the light switch. Samir tripped on a step and hit his left eyebrow on a hat stand. Özcan stumbled over Samir's feet and grabbed his back for support as he fell. Samir groaned under his weight. Manólis was still standing, but he had forgotten the flashlights.

Their eyes adjusted to the darkness. Samir wiped the blood off his face. Finally, Manólis found the light switch. The interior of the house was Japanese—Samir and Özcan just didn't see how anyone could live this way. It took them only a few minutes to locate the safe—the description they'd been given was a good one. They used crowbars to pry it out of the wall, then dragged it to the car. Manólis wanted to go back into the house—he'd discovered the kitchen and he was hungry. They argued about it for a long time, until Samir decided it was too dangerous. They could easily stop at a café on the way back. Manólis grumbled.

They tried to open the safe in a cellar in Neukölln. They had some familiarity with heavily armoured safes, but this one resisted them. Özcan had to borrow his brother-in-law's high-powered drill. Four hours later, when the safe opened, they knew it had been worth it. They found 120,000 euros in cash and six watches in a box. And there was also a small casket made of black lacquered wood. Samir opened it. It was lined with red silk and inside was an old bowl. Özcan thought it was hideous and wanted to throw it away, Samir wanted to give it to his sister, and Manólis didn't care—he was still hungry. Finally, they agreed to sell the bowl to Mike. Mike had a little shop with a big sign outside. He called himself an antiques dealer, but basically all he had was a small truck, and most of his business was clearing out apartments and dealing in junk. He paid them thirty euros for the bowl.

As they left the cellar, Samir clapped Özcan on the shoulder, said 'Özcan's Eleven' again, and they all laughed. Manólis's sister would get three thousand euros for her friend. Each of them had almost forty thousand euros in his pocket, and Samir would sell the watches to a fence. It had been a simple, clean break-in; there wouldn't be any problems.

They were wrong.

Hiroshi Tanata stood in his bedroom and looked at the hole in the wall. He was seventy-six years old. His family had left its mark on Japan for many hundreds of years; they were in insurance, banking and heavy industry. Tanata didn't cry out; he didn't wave his arms; he simply stared into the hole. But his secretary, who had served him for thirty years, told his wife that night that he had never seen Tanata in such a rage.

The secretary had a great deal to do that day. The police were in the house, asking questions. They suspected the employees—the alarm had certainly been switched off and there was no sign of forced entry—but their suspicions hadn't yet focused on anyone in particular. Tanata was standing up for his employees. The forensic investigation wasn't producing anything much, either. The technicians found no fingerprints, and there wasn't even a question of DNA evidence—the cleaning lady had done a thorough job before the police were called. The secretary knew his employer very well, and his answers to the officers were evasive and monosyllabic.

It was more important to get word to the press and the leading collectors: should the Tanata tea bowl be offered to anyone, the family who had owned it since the sixteenth century would pay the highest price for its return. In such an instance, all Mr Tanata would ask would be the name of the seller.

The hairdresser's on the Yorckstrasse had the same name as its owner: Pocol. The shop window displayed two faded advertising posters for styling products that dated from the 1980s: a blonde beauty in a striped sweater with too much hair and a man with a long chin and a moustache. Pocol had inherited the shop from his father. In his youth, Pocol had actually cut people's hair himself, having learned to do this at home. Now he ran some legal gambling joints and many more illegal ones. He kept the shop, sat all day in one of the comfortable tilting chairs, drank tea, and conducted his business. Over the years, he'd grown fat—he had a weakness for Turkish pastries. His brother-in-law owned a bakery three doors down and made the best *balli elmali*—honeyed apple fritters—in the city.

Pocol was short-tempered and brutal, and he knew that

this was the capital he traded on. Everyone had heard the story at least once about the café owner who'd told Pocol he should pay for what he ate. That was fifteen years ago. Pocol didn't know the café owner and the café owner didn't know Pocol. Pocol threw his food at the wall, went to the trunk of his car, and came back with a baseball bat. The landlord lost the sight in his right eye, his spleen, and his left kidney, and spent the rest of his life in a wheelchair. Pocol was sentenced to eight years for attempted murder. The day the sentence was handed down, the landlord fell down the stairs in the subway in his wheelchair, breaking his neck. After Pocol had served out his sentence, he never had to pay for another meal again.

Pocol read about the robbery in the newspaper. After a dozen phone calls to relatives, friends, fences and other business associates, he knew who'd broken into Tanata's house. He sent off a torpedo, an ambitious boy who did everything for him. The torpedo told Samir and Özcan that Pocol wanted to talk to them. Now.

The two of them showed up at the hairdresser's a short time later—you didn't make Pocol wait. There were pastries and tea; the atmosphere was friendly. Then suddenly Pocol began to scream, grabbed Samir by the hair, dragged him through the shop, threw him in a corner, and started kicking him. Samir didn't fight back, and between kicks he offered a cut of 30 percent. Pocol grunted, nodded, turned away from Samir, picked up a flat piece of wood he kept in the shop for things like this, and slammed Özcan in the forehead with it. After that, he calmed down, sat back in the tilting chair, and summoned his girlfriend from the room next door.

Pocol's girlfriend had still been working as a model a few months ago and had managed to be selected as *Playboy*'s September Playmate of the Month. She was dreaming of becoming a catwalk model or making it big with a music producer when Pocol discovered her, beat up her boyfriend, and became her manager. He called it 'plucking'. He arranged for her to have her breasts enlarged and her lips plumped. In the beginning, she believed in his plans, and Pocol really did try to get her taken on by an agency. When it became too much of an effort, there were appearances at discos, then strip clubs, and finally in the kind of extreme porno movies that were illegal in Germany. At some point, Pocol gave her her first shot of heroin, and now she was dependent on him and loved him. Pocol didn't have sex with her anymore, not since his friends had used her as a urinal in one of the movies. She was still around only because he wanted to sell her to Beirut—human trafficking also went on in that direction— and finally he needed to get back the money that had gone to the cosmetic surgeon.

The girlfriend bandaged Özcan's laceration, and Pocol made jokes about how he now looked like an Indian, 'Y'know, a redskin.' More tea and pastries appeared, the girlfriend was banished, and negotiations could proceed. The split was agreed at 50 percent, and Pocol would get the watches and the bowl. Samir and Özcan acknowledged their mistake, Pocol stressed that it was nothing personal, and as they said goodbye he hugged Samir and gave him a big kiss.

Shortly after the two of them had left the shop, Pocol called Wagner. Wagner was a liar and a con man. He was five feet two inches tall, his skin had turned yellow from years in tanning salons, and his hair was dyed brown, with a quarter of an inch of grey regrowth at the roots. Wagner's apartment was a 1980s cliché. It was a duplex; the bedroom, with its mirrored closets, flokati rugs and a gigantic bed, was on the upper floor. The living room downstairs was a landscape of white leather sofas, white marble floors, lacquered white walls and diamond-shaped side tables. Wagner loved everything shiny; even his mobile phone was encrusted with little pieces of glass.

Some years previously, he had declared personal bankruptcy, dividing his property among his relatives, and because justice in these matters is slow, he continued to accumulate debts. In fact, Wagner owned nothing anymore; the apartment belonged to his ex-wife, he hadn't been able to pay his medical insurance for months, and he still owed the beauty salon for his girlfriend's total makeover. The money he had earned so easily in earlier years had all been spent on cars and champagne and coke parties on Ibiza. Now the investment bankers he used to party with had all disappeared and he could no longer afford new tyres for his ten-year-old Ferrari. Wagner had spent a long time waiting for the big opportunity, the one that would make everything good again. In cafés, he told waitresses he needed a big one, and then roared with laughter every time over the hoary joke. Wagner had spent his whole life struggling with his own insignificance.

While the average con man just cons, Wagner was more skilled. He presented himself as the 'tough Berlin kid from the bottom' who'd 'made it'. Middle-class people put their trust in him. They thought he was rough, noisy and unpleasant but, for those very reasons, genuine and honourable. Wagner was neither hard nor honourable. He hadn't 'made it'—not even by his own standards. He was sly rather than intelligent, and because he was weak himself, he recognised the weaknesses in other people. He exploited these, even when it gained him no advantage.

Sometimes Pocol made use of Wagner. He beat him up when he got cheeky, when it was too long since the last time, or simply when he felt so inclined. Otherwise, he considered him to be garbage. But Wagner struck him as the right man for this job. Pocol had learned from experience that because of his origins and the way he spoke, nobody outside his own circle would take him seriously.

Wagner was given the task of getting in touch with Tanata to tell him he could buy back both bowl and watches, details to be sorted out later. Wagner agreed. He got hold of Tanata's phone number and talked for twenty minutes to the secretary. Wagner was assured that the police would not be brought into it. After he'd hung up, he felt terrific, stroked the two chihuahuas he'd named Dolce and Gabbana, and pondered how he could screw Pocol just a little in the bargain.

A garrotte is a thin length of wire with little wooden handles at either end. It was developed from a medieval instrument of torture and execution—until 1974, it was the official instrument of execution in Spain—and even today it is a favoured murder weapon. Its constituent parts can be bought at any hardware store; it's cheap, easy to transport, and effective: the wire is passed around the neck from behind and pulled tight into a noose; the victim cannot cry out, and death is swift.

Four hours after the phone call to Tanata, the doorbell rang at Wagner's apartment. Wagner opened the door a crack. The gun he'd stuck into the belt of his pants didn't save him. The first blow to his larynx cut off his breath, and when the garrotte ended his life fifteen minutes later, he welcomed his death.

Wagner's cleaning lady put down the groceries in the kitchen next morning and saw two severed fingers stuck in the sink. She called the police. Wagner was lying in bed, his thighs clamped together in a vise, two carpenter's nails in the left kneecap and three in the right. There was a garrotte around his neck and his tongue hung out of his mouth. Wagner had wet himself before he died, and the investigating officers racked their brains trying to figure out what information he had divulged to the perpetrator.

In the living room, where the marble floor met the wall, lay the two dogs; their yapping must have disturbed the visitor, who had stomped on them both. The trace analysts tried to get a print of the soles from the bodies, but it took the pathology people to locate a little fragment of plastic inside one of the dogs. The perpetrator had obviously worn plastic bags over his shoes.

During the same night that Wagner died, at around five o'clock in the morning Pocol carried the takings from his gambling dens into the hairdresser's in two plastic buckets. He was tired, and as he bent forward to unlock the door, he heard a high-pitched hum. He recognised it. His brain couldn't process it fast enough, but a fraction of a second before the ball at the end of the telescoping steel rod smashed against his head, he knew what it was.

His girlfriend found him in the shop when she came begging for heroin. He was lying face down on one of the two tilting chairs, his arms around it as if to embrace it. His hands were bound underneath it with zip ties; the massive body was jammed between the armrests. Pocol was naked, and the broken shaft of a broom was protruding out of his anus. The medical examiner testified at the autopsy that the force with which the stick had been inserted had also perforated the bladder. Pocol's body showed 117 lacerations on the back and head; the killer's steel ball had broken fourteen bones. Which one of the blows finally killed him could not be ascertained with any certainty. Pocol's safe had not been broken into, and the two buckets of coins from the slot machines stood almost undisturbed in the doorway. There was a coin in Pocol's mouth when he died, and another was found in his aesophagus.

The investigations went nowhere. The fingerprints in Pocol's shop could be attributed to any number of criminals in Neukölln and Kreuzberg. The torture with the broom handle pointed to Arab involvement, since they ranked it as a particular form of humiliation. There were a few arrests and interrogations of people who might be associated with it; the police thought it was a turf war, but they had nothing definite. Pocol and Wagner had never surfaced together in any police investigation and the homicide division could build no connection between the two cases. When it came down to it, there was only a pile of theories.

Pocol's shop and the footpath outside it were closed off with red-and-white security tape, and searchlights illuminated the area. Every single person in Neukölln who wanted to know found out during the on-site police investigation just how Pocol had died. And now Samir, Özcan and Manólis were truly frightened. At 11:00 a.m. they were standing in front of Pocol's shop with the money, the watches and the bowl. Mike, the antiques dealer they had sold the bowl to, was putting ice on his right eye four streets away. He had had to give back the bowl and pay a so-called 'expense allowance'. His black eye was part of it; those were the rules.

Manólis said what everyone was thinking: Pocol had been tortured, and if they had been part of the discussion, he would, of course, have given them up. If someone had felt confident enough to kill Pocol, their own lives were not going to be worth much. Samir said the thing with the bowl had to be settled, and quick. The others agreed, and finally Özcan thought maybe they should get a lawyer.

The three young men told me their story; that is to say, Manólis did the talking, but he kept wandering off into the philosophical and had trouble concentrating. The whole thing took quite some time. Then they said they weren't sure if Tanata knew who had done the break-in. They laid the money, the watches and the little lacquered casket with the tea bowl on the conference table and asked me to return the objects to the owner. I recorded everything as accurately as I could, and I refused to take the cash, as that would have been money laundering. I telephoned Tanata's secretary and arranged an appointment for that afternoon.

Tanata's house was on a quiet street in Dahlem. There was

no doorbell; an invisible electric eye triggered a signal, a dark gong sound, like something in a Zen monastery. The secretary gave me his card with both hands, fingers outstretched, which seemed a little pointless, since I was already there. Then I remembered that the exchange of cards is a ritual in Japan, and I reciprocated. The secretary was affable and serious. He led me to a room with earth-coloured walls and a floor of black wood. We seated ourselves at a table on hard stools; otherwise, the room was bare, except for a dark green ikebana arrangement in a niche in the wall. The indirect lighting was warm and subdued.

I opened my attaché case and laid out the objects. The secretary placed the watches on a leather tray that was standing ready, but he didn't touch the closed casket with the tea bowl. I asked him to sign the receipt I had prepared. He excused himself and disappeared behind a sliding door.

It was absolutely silent.

Then he came back, signed the receipt for the watches and the tea bowl, took the tray with him, and left me alone again. The casket remained unopened.

Tanata was a small man and looked desiccated somehow. He greeted me in the Western fashion, seemed in a good mood, and told me about his family in Japan.

After a time, he went to the table, opened the casket, and lifted out the bowl. He held it at the base with one hand and turned it slowly before his eyes with the other. It was a matcha bowl, in which gleaming green tea powder is beaten with a bamboo whisk. The bowl was black, with a glaze over its dark body. Such bowls were not turned on a wheel, but shaped by hand, and none of them resembled any other. The most ancient school of pottery signed its ceramics with the character raku. A friend had once told me that ancient Japan lived on in these bowls.

Tanata placed it carefully back in the casket and said, 'The bowl was made for our family by Chojiro in 1581.' Chojiro was the founder of the raku tradition. The bowl stared out of its red silk like a black eye. 'You know, there has already been a war over this bowl. It was a long time ago, and the war lasted almost five years. I'm glad things went quicker this time.' He let the lid of the casket snap shut. It echoed.

I said the money would also be repaid. He shook his head.

'What money?' he asked.

'The money in your safe.'

'There wasn't any money in there.'

I didn't understand him at first.

'My clients said—'

'If there had been any money in there,' he interrupted me, 'it might have been untaxed.'

'Yes?'

'And since a receipt would have to be presented to the police, questions would be asked. When the charges were presented, I never admitted that the money had been stolen.'

We finally agreed that I would inform the police of the return of the bowl and the watches. Naturally, Tanata did not ask me who the criminals were, and I didn't ask about Pocol and Wagner. Only the police asked questions; I was able to invoke the lawyer-client privilege to protect my clients.

Samir, Özcan and Manólis survived.

Samir received a call inviting him and his friends to a café on the Kurfürstendamm. The man who met them was polite. He showed them Pocol's and Wagner's dying minutes on his mobile-phone display, apologised for the quality of the images, and invited the three of them to share some cake with him. They didn't touch the cake, but next day they returned the 120,000 euros. They knew what was proper, and paid an additional 28,000 euros 'for expenses'; it was all they could raise. The friendly gentleman said it really wasn't necessary, and took the money.

Manólis retired, took over one of his family's restaurants, got married, and settled down. They say there are pictures of fjords and fishing boats in his restaurants, and Finnish vodka, and that he's planning to take his family and move to Finland.

Özcan and Samir turned to drug dealing; they never stole anything again that they couldn't classify.

Tanata's cleaning lady, who'd provided the tip that triggered the robbery, took a holiday in Anatolia two years later; she'd forgotten the whole thing long ago. She went swimming. Although the sea was calm that day, she hit her head on a rock and drowned.

I once saw Tanata again at the Philharmonic Hall in Berlin; he was sitting four rows behind me. When I turned around, he saluted me amicably but silently. Six months later, he was dead. His body was taken back to Japan, the house in Dahlem was sold, and his secretary also returned to his homeland.

The bowl is now the centerpiece of the Tanata Foundation Museum in Tokyo.

Postscript

When Manólis met Samir and Özcan, he was under suspicion for drug dealing. The suspicion was unfounded, and the court-ordered wire tap was disconnected shortly thereafter. But the first contact between Manólis and Samir was recorded. Özcan listened to it on the mobile phone's loudspeaker and joined in.

Samir: 'Are you Greek?'

Manólis: 'I'm a Finn.'

Samir: 'You don't sound like a Finn.'

Manólis: 'I'm a Finn.'

Samir: 'You sound like a Greek.'

Manólis: 'So what. Just because my mother and my father and my grandmothers and my grandfathers and everyone in my family are Greeks doesn't mean I have to run around my whole life being a Greek. I hate olive trees and tzatziki and that idiotic dance. I'm Finnish. Every particle of me is Finnish. I'm an inner Finn.'

Özcan to Samir: 'He also looks like a Greek.'

Samir to Özcan: 'Let him be a Finn if he wants to be a Finn.'

Özcan to Samir: 'He doesn't even look Swedish.' (Özcan knew a Swede from school.)

Samir: 'Why are you a Finn?'

Manólis: 'Because of the thing with the Greeks.'

Samir: 'Huh?'

Özcan: 'Huh?'

Manólis: 'It's been going on for hundreds of years with the Greeks. Imagine there's a ship going down.'

Özcan: 'Why?'

Manólis: 'Because it's sprung a leak or the captain's drunk.'

Özcan: 'But why has the ship sprung a leak?'

Manólis: 'Shit, it's only an example.'

Özcan: 'Hmm.'

Manólis: 'The ship's just sinking, okay?'

Özcan: 'Hmm.'

Manólis: 'Everyone drowns. Everyone. Got it? Only one Greek survives. He swims and swims and swims and eventually makes it to shore. He pukes all the salt water out of his throat. He pukes out of his mouth. Out of his nose. Out of every pore. He spits it all out, until he eventually falls asleep, half-dead. The guy is the only survivor. All the rest of them are dead. He lies on the beach and sleeps. When he wakes up, he realises he's the only one who's survived. So he stands up and slays the next person he meets who's out for a walk. Just like that. Only when the other guy is dead is everything evened out.'

Samir: 'Huh?'

Özcan: 'Huh?'

Manólis: 'D'you understand? He has to kill someone else, so that the one who didn't drown is dead, too. The other guy has to stand in for him. Minus one, plus one. Get it?'

Samir: 'No.'

Özcan: 'Where was the leak?'

Samir: 'When are we going to meet?'

The Cello

Tackler's dinner jacket was light blue, his shirt pink. His double chin overflowed both collar and bow tie; his jacket strained over his stomach and made folds across his chest. He stood between his daughter Theresa and his fourth wife, both of whom towered over him. The black-haired fingers of his left hand clutched his daughter's hip. They lay there like a dark animal.

The reception had cost him a lot of money, but he felt it had been worth it, because they had all come: the first minister of the state, the bankers, the powerful and the beautiful and, most important of all, the famous music critic. That was all he wanted to think about right now. It was Theresa's party.

Theresa was twenty at the time, a classical slender beauty with an almost perfectly symmetrical face. She seemed calm and composed, and only a little vein in her neck betrayed how fast her heart was beating.

After a short speech by her father, she took her seat on the red-carpeted stage and tuned her cello. Her brother Leonhard sat next to her on a stool to turn the pages of the sheet music. The contrast between the two of them could not have been greater. Leonhard was a head shorter than Theresa; he had inherited his father's features and physique but not his toughness. Sweat ran down his red face into his shirt; the edge of his collar had darkened with it. He smiled out at the audience, friendly and softhearted.

The guests sat on tiny chairs. They gradually fell silent, and the lights were dimmed. And while I was still deciding whether I was in fact going to leave the garden and go back into the salon, she began to play. She played the first three of Bach's six cello suites, and after a few bars I realised I would never be able to forget Theresa. On that warm summer evening in the grand salon of the nineteenth-century villa, with its tall mullioned glass doors opened wide onto the park that was all lit up, I experienced one of those rare moments of absolute happiness that only music can give us.

Tackler was a second-generation building contractor. He and his father were self-assertive, intelligent men who'd made their money in Frankfurt with real estate. All his life, his father had carried a revolver in his right trouser pocket and a roll of cash in the left. Tackler no longer needed a weapon.

Three years after Leonhard was born, his mother visited one of her husband's new high-rise buildings. The topping-out ceremony was taking place on the eighteenth floor. Someone had forgotten to secure a parapet. The last Tackler saw of his wife was her handbag and a champagne glass, which she had set down next to her on a table.

In the years that followed, a whole cavalcade of 'mothers' paraded past the children. None of them stayed longer than three years. Tackler ran a prosperous home; there was a driver, a cook, a whole series of cleaning women, and two gardeners for the park. He didn't have time to occupy himself with his children's upbringing, so the one constant in their lives was an elderly nurse. She had already brought up Tackler, smelled of lavender, and was known to one and all simply as Etta. Her main interest was ducks. In her two-room attic apartment in Tackler's house, she had hung five stuffed specimens on the walls, and even the brown felt hat she always wore when she went out had two blue drake's feathers tucked into the band. Children didn't especially appeal to her.

Etta had always stayed; she'd long ago become one of the family. Tackler considered childhood a waste of time and barely remembered his own. He trusted Etta, because she agreed with him about the fundamentals of child rearing. They should grow up with discipline and without what Tackler called 'conceit'. Sometimes severity was required.

Theresa and Leonhard had to earn their own pocket money. In summer, they weeded dandelions in the garden and received a ha'penny for each plant—'but only with its roots; otherwise you get nothing,' said Etta. She counted the individual plants as meanly as she counted the pennies. In winter, they had to shovel snow. Etta paid by the yard.

When Leonhard was nine, he ran away from the house. He climbed a pine tree in the park and waited for them to come searching for him. He imagined first Etta and then his father despairing and lamenting his flight. Nobody despaired. Before supper, Etta called that if he didn't come right now, there would be nothing more to eat and he'd get his bottom smacked. Leonhard gave up. His clothes were full of resin, and he was given a slap on the ears.

At Christmas, Tackler gave the children soap and pullovers. There was only one time when a business friend, who'd made a lot of money with Tackler in the course of the year, gave Leonhard a toy gun and Theresa a doll's kitchen. Etta took the toys down to the cellar. 'They don't need that sort of thing,' she said, and Tackler, who hadn't been listening, agreed.

Etta considered their upbringing complete when brother and sister could behave themselves at the table, speak proper German, and otherwise keep quiet. She told Tackler she thought they'd come to a bad end. They were too soft, not real Tacklers like him and his father. It was a sentence he remembered.

Etta got Alzheimer's, slowly regressed, and became gentler. She left her birds to a museum of local history, which had no use for them and ordered the stuffed creatures destroyed. Tackler and the two children were the only ones at her funeral. On the way back, he said, 'So, now that's out of the way.'

Leonhard worked for Tackler during the holidays. He would rather have gone off with friends, but he had no money. That was how Tackler wanted it. He took his son to one of the building sites, handed him over to the foreman, and told him to 'really let him have it'. The foreman did what he could, and when Leonhard threw up at the end of the second day from exhaustion, Tackler said he'd get used to it. He himself had sometimes slept on building sites with his father when he was Leonhard's age and shat in the open air like the other bar benders. Leonhard shouldn't get any ideas he was 'better' than the others.

Theresa had holiday jobs, too; she worked in the company bookkeeping department. Like Leonhard, she received only 30 percent of the average salary. 'You're no help; you actually create work. Your pay is a gift, not something you've earned,' said Tackler. If they wanted to go to the movies, Tackler gave the two of them a total of ten euros, and since they had to take the bus, it was only enough for one ticket. They didn't dare tell him that. Sometimes Tackler's driver took them into town secretly and gave them a little money— he had children himself and knew his boss.

Other than Tackler's sister, who was employed in the company and had always given up every one of her secrets to her brother since her own childhood, there were no relatives. The children began by fearing their father, then hated him, until finally his world became so alien to them that they had nothing more to say to him.

Tackler didn't despise Leonhard, but he loathed his softness. He thought he had to harden him; 'forge' him was the way he put it. When Leonhard was fifteen, he put up a picture in his room of a ballet production he had gone to with his class. Tackler tore it off the wall and roared at him that he'd better be careful or he'd be turning gay. He was too fat, Tackler said to Leonhard; he'd never get a girlfriend like that.

Theresa spent every minute with her cello and her music

teacher in Frankfurt. Tackler didn't understand her, so he left her in peace—with one exception. It was summertime, shortly after Theresa's sixteenth birthday. She went skinny-dipping in the pool. When she came out of the water, Tackler was standing at the edge. He'd been drinking. He looked at her as if she were a stranger, picked up the towel, and began to dry her. As he touched her breasts, he smelled of whiskey. She ran into the house. She never used the pool again.

On the rare occasions they all had dinner together, conversation revolved around his themes of watches, food and cars. Theresa and Leonhard knew the price of every car and every famous make of watch. It was an abstract game. Sometimes their father showed them financial statements, stock market and business reports. 'This will all belong to you someday,' he said, and Theresa whispered to Leonhard that he was quoting from a movie. 'The inner self,' he said, 'is nonsense.' It gained no one anything.

All the children had was each other. When Theresa was accepted at the conservatory, they decided they would both leave their father together. They wanted to tell him at dinner and had rehearsed it, working out how he would react and what their responses should be. When they began, Tackler said he didn't have time today, and disappeared. They had to wait for three weeks; then Theresa took the lead. The two of them thought that if she were the one, Tackler would at least be unable to hit her. She said they were both going to leave Bad Homburg now. 'Leave Bad Homburg' sounded better, they thought, than saying it directly. Theresa said she was going to take Leonhard with her, that they would make their way somehow.

Tackler didn't understand, and kept eating. When he asked Theresa to pass him the bread, Leonhard screamed, 'You've tortured us enough,' and Theresa, more quietly, said, 'We don't ever want to become like you.' Tackler let his knife drop onto his plate. It echoed. Then he stood up without a word, went to his car, and drove to his girlfriend's. It was almost 3:00 a.m. when he returned.

Later that same night, Tackler sat alone in the library. A silent home movie was running on the screen he'd had built into the bookshelves. It had been transferred to video from a Super-8 camera. The footage was overexposed.

His first wife is holding the two children by the hand; Theresa is probably three years old and Leonhard two. His wife says something; her mouth moves soundlessly. She lets go of Theresa's hand and points into the distance. The camera follows her arm; there is the ruin of a castle in the blurry background. Pan back to Leonhard, who hides himself behind his mother's leg and cries. Stones and grass blur in the foreground; the camera is passed to someone else while it's still running. It pans upward again, showing Tackler in jeans and an open shirt, his chest hair exposed. He roars with soundless laughter, he holds Theresa up to the sun, he kisses her, he waves to the camera. The image flares and the film breaks off.

That night, Tackler decided to arrange a farewell concert for Theresa. His contacts should suffice; he would 'put her right on top'. Tackler didn't want to be a bad person. He wrote each of his children a cheque for 250,000 euros and put them on the breakfast table. He felt that was enough.

The day after the concert, there was an article in the regional newspaper that bordered on the euphoric. The great music critic certified that Theresa had a 'brilliant future' as a musician.

She didn't register at the conservatory. Theresa believed her gift to be so great that she could still take her time. For now, it was something else that mattered. The two of them spent most of the next three years travelling through Europe and the United States. She gave a few private concerts and otherwise played only for her brother. Tackler's money made them independent, at least for a while. They remained inseparable. They took none of their love affairs seriously, and there was scarcely a day in those years that either of them spent away from the other. They seemed to be free.

Almost two years to the day after her concert in Bad Homburg, I encountered the two of them again at a party near Florence, in the Castello di Tornano, a ruined castle from the eleventh century, surrounded by olive trees and cypresses amid the vineyards. The host described them both as 'gilded youth' when they arrived in a 1960s convertible sports car. Theresa kissed him and Leonhard doffed his idiotic Borsalino straw hat with studied elegance.

When I told Theresa later that I had never heard the cello suites performed with more intensity than in her father's house, she said, 'It's the prelude to the first suite. Not the sixth, which everyone thinks is the most important and is the most difficult. No, it's the first.' She took a mouthful of wine, leaned forward, and whispered in my ear, 'D'you understand, the prelude to the first. It's all of life packed into three minutes.' Then she laughed.

At the end of the following summer, the two of them were in Sicily. They spent a few days with a commodities trader who had rented a house there for the summer and was somewhat infatuated with Theresa.

Leonhard woke up with a light fever. He thought it was due to the alcohol of the previous night. He didn't want to be ill, not on a glorious day like this, not when they were having the time of their lives. The *E. coli* bacteria colonised his body at great speed. They had been in the water he'd drunk at a petrol station two days before.

They found an old Vespa in the garage and were headed toward the sea. The apple was lying in the middle of the asphalt; it had fallen off one of the harvest trucks. It was almost round and glinted in the noonday light. Theresa said something, and Leonhard turned his head to hear her properly. The front wheel went over the apple and slid sideways. Leonhard lost control. Theresa was lucky; she only sprained her shoulder and had a couple of abrasions. Leonhard's head got wedged between the back wheel and a boulder and burst open.

During the first night in the hospital, his condition deteriorated. Nobody tested his blood; there were other things to do. Theresa called her father and he used the corporate Learjet to send a doctor from Frankfurt; the man arrived too late. Leonhard's kidneys had released their poison into his bloodstream. Theresa sat in the waiting area outside the operating theatre. The doctor held her hand as he spoke to her. The air conditioning was loud, and the pane of glass Theresa had been staring at for hours was clouded with dust. The doctor said it was a sepsis of the urinary tract, engendering multiple organ failures. Theresa didn't understand what he was telling her. Urine had spread through Leonhard's body, and he had a 20 percent chance of survival. The doctor kept talking, and his words gave her some distance. Theresa had not slept for almost forty hours. When he went back into the operating room, she closed her eyes. He had said 'decease,' and she saw the word in front of her in black letters. They had nothing to do with her brother. She said, 'No.' Just 'No.' Nothing else.

On the sixth day after Leonhard's admission to hospital, his condition stabilised. He could be flown to Berlin. When he was admitted to the Charité Hospital, his body was covered with black, leathery, necrotic patches that indicated the death of cellular tissue. The doctors operated fourteen times. The thumb, forefinger and fourth finger of the left hand were amputated. The left toes were cut off at the joint, as was the front half of the right foot and parts of the back. All that remained was a deformed lump that could barely support any weight, with bones and cartilage pressing visibly against the skin.

Leonhard lay in an artificially induced coma. He had survived, but the effects of the injury to his head could not yet be measured.

The hippocampus is Poseidon's pack animal, a Greek sea monster, half horse, half worm. It gives its name to a very ancient part of the brain within the temporal lobe. It's where the work is done that transforms short-term memories into long-term ones. Leonhard's hippocampus had been damaged. When he was revived from the coma after nine weeks, he asked Theresa who she was and then who he was. He had lost all power of recall and couldn't hold on to any perception for longer than three or four minutes. After endless tests, the doctors tried to explain to him that it was amnesia, both anterograde and retrograde. Leonhard understood their explanations, but after three minutes and forty seconds he had forgotten them again. He also forgot the fact that he forgot.

And when Theresa was tending him, all he saw was a beautiful woman.

After two months, they were able to move together into their father's Berlin apartment. Every day a nurse came for three hours and otherwise Theresa took care of everything. At first, she still invited friends to come for dinner; then she ceased to be able to bear the way they looked at Leonhard. Tackler came to see them once a month.

They were lonely months. Gradually, Theresa deteriorated; her hair turned to straw and her skin lost its colour. One evening, she took the cello out of its case; she hadn't touched it for months. She played in the half darkness of the room. Leonhard was lying on the bed, dozing. At a certain point, he pushed off the bedclothes and began to masturbate. She stopped playing and turned away to the window. He asked her to come to him. Theresa looked at him. He sat up, asked to kiss her. She shook her head. He let himself fall back and said at least she could unbutton her blouse. The scarred stump of his right foot lay on the white sheet like a lump of flesh. She went to him and stroked his cheek. Then she took off her clothes, sat down on the chair, and played with her eyes closed. She waited until he fell asleep, stood up, used a towel to wipe the sperm off his stomach, covered him up, and kissed his forehead.

She went into the bathroom and vomited.

Although the doctors had ruled out any possibility that Leonhard could recover his memory, the cello seemed to move him. When she was playing, she seemed to feel a pale, almost imperceptible connection to her former life, a weak reflection of the intensity she missed so much. Sometimes Leonhard actually remembered the cello the next day. He talked about it, and even if he couldn't make any connections, something did seem to remain captured in his memory. Theresa now played for him every evening, he almost always masturbated, and she almost always collapsed in the bathroom afterward and wept.

Six months after the last operation, Leonhard's scars began to hurt. The doctors said further amputations would be required. After doing a PET scan, they told her he would also soon lose the power of speech. Theresa knew that she wouldn't be able to bear it.

The twenty-sixth of November was a cold, grey autumn day; darkness came early. Theresa had put candles on the table and pushed Leonhard to his place in his wheelchair. She had bought the ingredients for the fish soup in Berlin's best market; he had always liked it. The soup, the peas, the venison roast, the chocolate mousse, even the wine were all laced with Luminal, a barbiturate she had no problem obtaining to treat Leonhard's pain. She gave it to him in small amounts so that he wouldn't vomit it up again. She herself ate nothing and waited.

Leonhard grew sleepy. She pushed him into the bathroom and ran water in the big tub. She undressed him. He barely had the strength anymore to haul himself into the tub by using the new handles. Then she took off her own clothes and got into the warm water with him. He sat in front of her, his head leaning back on her breasts, breathing calmly and steadily. As children, they had often sat in the bath this way, because Etta didn't want to waste water. Theresa held him in a tight embrace, her head on his shoulder. When he had fallen asleep, she kissed his neck and let him slide under the surface. Leonhard breathed in deeply. There was no death struggle; the Luminal had disabled his capacity to control his muscles. His lungs filled with water and he drowned. His head lay between her legs, his eyes were closed, and his long hair floated on the surface. After two hours, she climbed out of the cold bath, covered her dead brother with a towel, and called me.

She confessed, but it was no mere confession. She sat for more than seven hours in front of the two investigators and dictated her life onto the record. She rendered an account of herself. She began with her childhood and ended with the death of her brother. She left nothing out. She didn't cry; she didn't break down. She sat as straight as a die and spoke steadily, calmly, and in polished sentences. There was no need for intervening questions. While her statement was being typed up, we smoked a cigarette in an adjoining room. She said she wasn't going to talk about it anymore; she had said all there was to say. 'I don't have anything else,' she said.

Naturally, she was ordered to be detained because of the murder charge. I visited her almost every day in prison. She arranged for books to be sent in, and didn't leave her cell even when the prisoners had their yard exercise. Reading was her anaesthetic. When we met, she didn't want to talk about her brother. Nor did the imminent trial interest her. She preferred to read to me from her books, things she'd sought out in her cell. It was like a series of lectures in a prison. I liked her warm voice, but at the time I didn't understand: it was the only way she had left to express herself.

On the twenty-fourth of December, I was with her until the end of visiting time. Then they locked the bulletproof glass doors behind me. Outside, it had been snowing. Everything was peaceful; it was Christmas. Theresa was taken back to her cell; she sat down at the little table and wrote a letter to her father. Then she tore the bedsheet, wound it into a rope, and hanged herself from the window handle.

On the twenty-fifth of December, Tackler received a call from the lawyer on duty. After he'd put down the phone he opened the safe, took out his father's revolver, put the barrel in his mouth, and pulled the trigger.

The prison administration placed Theresa's belongings in the house vault for safekeeping. Under our powers of criminal procedure, we lawyers have the right to receive objects on behalf of our clients. At some point, the authorities sent a package of her clothes and her books. We forwarded it to her aunt in Frankfurt.

I kept one of her books; she had written my name on the flyleaf. It was F. Scott Fitzgerald's *The Great Gatsby*. The book lay untouched in my desk for two years before I could pick it up again. She had marked the passages she wanted to read to me in blue, and drawn tiny little staves of music notes next to them. Only one place was marked in red, the last sentence, and when I read it, I can still hear her voice:

So we beat on, boats against the current, borne back ceaselessly into the past.

The Hedgehog

The judges put on their robes in the conference room, one of the jury arrived a few minutes too late, and the constable was replaced after he complained of a toothache. The accused was a heavily built Lebanese man, Walid Abu Fataris, and he was silent from the very beginning. The witnesses testified, the victim exaggerated a little, and the evidence was analysed. The case being heard was that of a perfectly normal robbery, which normally carries a sentence of five to fifteen years. The judges were in agreement: given the previous record of the accused, they would give him eight years; there was no question about his guilt or his criminal responsibility. The trial babbled on all day. Nothing special, then, but there had been no expectation of that anyhow.

It turned three o'clock and the time for the main hearing would soon be over. There wasn't much left to do for today. The judge looked at the witness list; only Karim, a brother of the accused, was still to be heard. Hmmm, thought the presiding judge, we all know what to expect from alibis provided by relatives, and he eyed the witness over his reading glasses. He had only one question for this witness—namely, if he actually did mean to assert that his brother Walid had been at home when the pawnshop on the Wartenstrasse was looted. The judge put the question to Karim as simply as possible; he even asked twice if Karim had understood it.

No one had expected that Karim would even open his mouth. The presiding judge had explained to him at length that, as the brother of the accused, he had the right to remain silent. Now they were all waiting to see what he would do; his brother's future might hang on it. The judge was impatient, the lawyer bored, and one of the jury kept staring at the clock because he wanted to make the 5:00 p.m. train to Dresden. Karim was the last witness in this main hearing, the minor ones would get heard by the court at the end. Karim knew what he was doing. He'd always known.

Karim grew up in a family of criminals. It was a much-told tale about his uncle that he'd shot six men in Lebanon over a crate of tomatoes. Each of Karim's eight brothers had a record that took up to half an hour to read out in court at any trial. They had stolen, robbed, pulled con tricks, blackmailed and committed perjury. The only things for which they hadn't yet been found guilty were murder and manslaughter.

For generations in this family, cousins had married cousins and nephews had married nieces. When Karim started school, the teachers groaned—'Yet another Abu Fataris'—and then treated him like an idiot. He was made to sit in the back row, and his first-grade teacher told him, at age six, that he wasn't to draw attention to himself, get into fights, or talk at all. So Karim didn't say a word. It quickly became clear to him that he must not show he was different. His brothers smacked him on the back of the head because they didn't understand what he said. That is, if he was lucky. His classmates—thanks to a municipal integration plan, the first grade consisted of 80 percent foreigners—made fun of him when he tried to explain things to them. And just like his brothers, they, too, usually hit him whenever he seemed too different. So Karim deliberately set out to get bad grades. It was the only thing he could do.

By the time he was ten years old, he had taught himself stochastic theory, integral calculus and analytical geometry from a textbook. He had stolen the book from the teachers' library. As for class work, he had figured out how many of the ridiculous exercises he had to get wrong in order to be awarded an inconspicuous C2. Sometimes he had the feeling that his brain buzzed when he came upon a mathematical problem in the book that was reputed to be insoluble. Those were the moments that defined his personal happiness.

He lived, as did all his brothers, even the eldest of them, who was twenty-six, with his mother; his father had died shortly after he was born. The family apartment in Neukölln had six rooms. Six rooms for ten people. He was the youngest, so he got the box room. The skylight was made of milky glass and there was a set of pine shelves. This space was where things found a home after no one wanted them anymore: broomheads without broomsticks, buckets without handles, cables for appliances now lost and forgotten. He sat there all day in front of a computer, and while his mother assumed he'd be busying himself with video games like his big strong brothers, he was reading the classics on Gutenberg.org.

When he was twelve, he made his last attempt to be like his brothers. He wrote a program that could override the electronic firewalls in the post office savings bank and unobtrusively debit a matter of hundredths of a cent from millions of accounts. His brothers didn't understand what 'the moron', as they called him, had given them. They smacked him on the back of the head again and threw away the CD with the program on it. Walid was the only one to sense that Karim outclassed them, and he protected him against his cruder brothers.

When Karim turned eighteen, he finished school. He had made sure that he would barely pass his final exams. No one in his family had ever gotten that far. He borrowed eight thousand euros from Walid. Walid thought Karim needed the money for a drug deal and gave it to him gladly. Karim, in the meantime, had learned so much about the stock market that he was trading on the foreign-exchange market. Within a year, he had earned almost 700,000 euros. He rented a little apartment in a nice part of the city, left his family's place every morning, and took endless roundabout routes to be sure no one was following him. He furnished his refuge, bought books on mathematics and a faster computer, and spent his time trading on the stock exchange and reading.

His family, assuming 'the moron' was now dealing dope, was content. Of course he was far too slight to be a true Abu Fataris. Karim never went to the kickboxing and extreme-sports club, but he always wore gold chains like the others, and satin shirts in garish colours, and black nappa leather jackets. He talked Neukölln slang and even earned a little respect for never having been arrested. His brothers didn't take him seriously. If they'd been asked about him, the answer would have been simply that he was part of the family. Beyond that, nobody thought about him twice.

Karim's double life went unnoticed. No one was aware either that he owned a completely different set of clothes or that he'd used night school for fun to sail through his school-graduation certificate and attended lectures in mathematics twice a week at the Technical University. He had a small but significant fortune, he paid his taxes, and had a nice girl-friend, who was studying comparative literature and knew nothing about Neukölln.

Karim had read the charges against Walid. Everyone in the family had seen them, but he was the only one who under-stood their significance. Walid had raided a pawnbroker, robbed him of 14,490 euros, and raced home to establish an alibi. The victim had called the police and given them an exact description of the perpetrator; it was immediately clear to the two investigators that it had to be one of the Abu Fataris family. The brothers looked almost unbelievably alike, a circumstance that had already saved them more than once. No eyewitness could tell them apart at a lineup, and even tapes from security cameras didn't pick up much difference.

This time, the policemen moved fast. Walid had hidden the loot on his way back and thrown his weapon into the

River Spree. When the police stormed the apartment, he was sitting on the sofa, drinking tea. He was wearing an apple green T-shirt with the luminous yellow slogan FORCED TO WORK on it in English. He didn't know what it meant, but he liked it. The police arrested him. On the grounds of 'imminent danger', they made a mess of a search warrant, slicing open the sofas, emptying drawers onto the floor, overturning cupboards, and even ripping the skirting boards off the walls on the suspicion that these might conceal hiding places. They found nothing.

But Walid remained under arrest—the pawnbroker had described his T-shirt exactly. The two policemen were pleased to finally have picked up an Abu Fataris who could be put away for at least five years.

Karim sat in the witness chair and looked up at the judges' bench. He knew that nobody in the courtroom would believe a word he said if he merely gave Walid an alibi; when it came down to it, he was an Abu Fataris, one of the family pursued by the prosecutor's office as major repeat criminals. Everyone here expected him to lie. That wouldn't work. Walid would be swallowed up in the prison system for years.

Karim recited to himself the saying of Archilochus, the slave's son, which was his guiding motto: 'The fox knows many things, the hedgehog only one thing.' The judges and the prosecutors might be foxes, but he was the hedgehog and he'd learned his skills.

'Your Honour…' he said with a catch in his voice. He knew this wouldn't move anyone, but it would raise the

general level of attention a little. He was making an enormous
effort to sound stupid but sincere. 'Your Honour, Walid was
at home all evening.' He let the pause linger as he saw out of
the corner of his eye that the prosecutor was writing a provi-
sion that would be the basis of a legal proceeding against him
for perjury.

'So, indeed, at home all evening...' said the presiding
judge, and leaned forward. 'But the victim identified Walid
unequivocally.'

The prosecutor shook his head, and the defence lawyer
buried himself in his papers.

Karim knew the photos of the scene of the arrest from
the files. Four policemen who looked exactly like policemen:
little blond moustaches, pouches, bum bags, sneakers. And
then there was Walid: a head taller and twice as broad in the
shoulders, dark-skinned, green T-shirt with yellow writing.
A ninety-year-old half-blind lady, who hadn't been there,
could have 'identified him unequivocally'.

Karim's voice caught again, and he wiped his sleeve
across his nose. It came away with little things stuck to it.
He looked at it and said, 'No, Your Honour, it wasn't Walid.
Please believe me.'

'I remind you once again that when you testify here, you
are under an oath to tell the truth.'

'But I am.'

'You are risking severe punishment. You could go to jail,'
said the judge, wanting to issue a caution that would be on
Karim's level. Then he said rather superciliously, 'And who
would it have been if it wasn't Walid?' He looked around and
the prosecutor smiled.

'Indeed, who was it?' the prosecutor echoed, which earned him a punishing look from the presiding judge, because this was *his* turn to examine the witness.

Karim hesitated for as long as he could, counting silently to five. Then he said, 'Imad.'

'What? What do you mean, Imad?'

'That it was Imad, not Walid,' said Karim.

'And who is this Imad?'

'Imad is my other brother,' said Karim.

The presiding judge looked at him in amazement, and even the defence lawyer suddenly woke up again. An Abu Fataris breaks all the rules and incriminates someone else in his own family? they were all asking themselves.

'But Imad left before the police got there,' Karim added.

'Oh yes?' The presiding judge was beginning to get angry. Idiotic babble, he was thinking.

'He gave me this thing here,' said Karim. Knowing his testimony wasn't going to change anything, he had begun months before the trial to withdraw varying amounts of money from his accounts. Now that money, in the exact same denominations that Walid had stolen, was in a brown envelope, and he passed it to the judge.

'What's in it?' the judge asked.

'I don't know,' said Karim.

The judge tore open the envelope and pulled out the money. He wasn't thinking about fingerprints, but there wouldn't have been any anyway. He counted slowly out loud: 'Fourteen thousand four hundred and ninety euros. And Imad gave you this on the night of the seventeenth of April?'

'Yes, Your Honour, he did.'

The presiding judge paused for thought. Then he posed the question that he hoped would entrap this Karim person. With a certain undertone of contempt, he asked, 'You, the witness, can you remember what Imad was wearing when he gave you the envelope?'

'Ahhh … Just a moment.'

General relief on the judges' bench. The presiding judge leaned back.

Go slow, work a pause in there, and make yourself hesitate, thought Karim; then he said, 'Jeans, black leather jacket, T-shirt.'

'What kind of T-shirt?'

'Oh, I really don't remember,' said Karim.

The presiding judge looked smugly at the court reporter, who would have to write up the judgment later. The two judges nodded at each other.

'Ahhh…' Karim scratched his head. 'Oh, hold on, yes I do. We all got these T-shirts from our uncle. He got a great deal on them from somewhere and gave them to us. There's something on them in English, that we're supposed to work and so on. Really funny.'

'Do you mean this T-shirt that your brother Walid is wearing in the photograph?' The presiding judge showed Karim a picture from the folder of photographs.

'Yes, yes, Your Honour. Exactly. That's the one. We've got a whole ton of them. I'm wearing one, too. But that's Walid, not Imad, in the photo.'

'Yes, I know that,' said the judge.

'Show us,' said the prosecutor.

Finally, thought Karim, and said, 'Show how? They're in the apartment.'

'No, I mean the one you're wearing now.'

'Right now?' asked Karim.

When the prosecutor nodded solemnly, Karim shrugged and opened the zipper on his leather jacket as indifferently as he could. He was wearing the same T-shirt as Walid in the picture in the files. Karim had ordered twenty of them the previous week from one of the countless copy shops in Kreuzberg, handed them out to all his brothers, and left ten more in his family's apartment, just in case there would be a further search.

Court was recessed and Karim sent outside. But before that, he heard the judge say to the prosecutor that all they had left was a direct confrontation; they had no other proof. The first round went well, he thought.

When Karim was called back in again, he was asked if he had ever had a previous conviction, and he said no. The prosecutor's office had secured an extract from the criminal register to confirm this.

'Mr Abu Fataris,' said the prosecutor, 'you must be aware of the fact that your statement incriminates Imad.'

Karim nodded. Shamefaced, he looked at his shoes.

'Why are you doing this?'

'Well'—he was even stuttering a little by this point—'Walid is my brother, too. I'm the youngest; they all keep saying I'm the moron and so on. But Walid and Imad are both my brothers. Do you see? And if it was another brother, Walid can't end up in the can because of Imad. It would be better if it was someone quite different—I mean not one of the family—but it's one of my brothers. Imad, and so on.'

And now Karim went for the coup de grâce.

'Your Honour,' he said. 'It wasn't Walid, honest. But it's true, Walid and Imad look exactly like. See…' And he pulled a creased photo out of his greasy wallet with all nine brothers on it and held it out uncomfortably close to the presiding judge's nose. The judge reached for it irritably and laid it on his table.

'There, the first one right there, that's me. The second, that's Walid, Your Honour. The third one's Farouk, the fourth one's Imad, the fifth one's—'

'May we keep the photograph?' asked the court-appointed defence counsel, interrupting; he was a friendly, older lawyer and suddenly the case didn't look anything like so hopeless.

'Only if I can get it back; it's the only one I have. We had it taken for Auntie Halima in Lebanon. Six months ago, sort of all nine of us brothers together, you get it?' Karim looked at the members of the court to be sure that they got it. 'So Auntie could see all of us. But then we didn't send it, because Farouk said he looked stupid in it.' Karim looked at the picture again. 'He does look stupid in it, Farouk, I mean. He's not even—'

The presiding judge waved him off. 'Witness, go back to your chair.'

Karim sat down in the witness's chair and started over again. 'But see, Your Honour, the first one there, that's me, the second one's Walid, the third one's Farouk, the fourth—'

'Thank you,' said the judge, exasperated. 'We understood you.'

'Well, everyone gets them mixed up; even in school the

teachers couldn't tell them apart. Once they were doing this exam in biology class, and Walid was really bad in biology, so they...' Karim plowed on, undeterred.

'Thank you,' said the judge loudly.

'Nah, I need to tell you about the biology thing, the way it went was—'

'No,' said the judge.

Karim was dismissed as a witness and left the courtroom.

The pawnbroker was sitting on the spectators' bench. The court had already heard him, but he wanted to be there for the verdict. He was, after all, the victim. Now he was called to the front again and shown the family photo. He had understood it was all about number two, that he had to recognise him. He said—rather too quickly, as he himself acknowledged later—that the perpetrator was 'the second man in the picture, naturally'. He had no doubt that man was the perpetrator; yes, it was completely clear. 'Number two.' The court settled down a little.

Outside the door, Karim was wondering meantime how long it would take for the judges to get a handle on the situation. The presiding judge wouldn't need that much time; he would decide to question the pawnbroker again. Karim waited exactly four minutes and then went back, unsummoned, into the courtroom. He saw the pawnbroker at the judges' table, standing over the photograph. Everything was going the way he'd planned. Then he burst out that there was something he'd forgotten. They had to hear him again, please, just quickly; it was really important. The presiding judge, who had an aversion to interruptions like this, snapped, 'So now what?'

'Excuse me, I made a mistake, a really dumb mistake, Your Honour, just stupid.'

Karim was immediately the centre of attention of the entire courtroom again. They were all expecting him to withdraw his accusation against Imad. It happened all the time.

'*Imad*, Your Honour, it's *Imad* that's the second one in the picture. Walid isn't number two, he's number four. I'm so sorry; I'm just all muddled up. The questions and everything. Please excuse me.'

The presiding judge shook his head, the pawnbroker turned red, and the defence counsel grinned. 'The second, yes?' said the judge in a fury. 'So the second—'

'Yes, yes, the second. You see, Your Honour,' said Karim, 'we wrote on the back who everyone was, for Auntie, so that she'd know, because she—Auntie, I mean—doesn't know all of us. She wanted to see us together, just once, but she can't come to Germany, because of Immigration and stuff, you know. But there are so many of us brothers. Your Honour, turn the picture over. You see? All the names are right there in a row, in the same order they are on the front, in the picture. And when can I get it back?'

After they'd pulled slides of Imad out of the files and examined them, the court had to let Walid go.

Imad was arrested. But, as Karim knew perfectly well, he had stamps in his passport for both arrival and exit, proving that he'd been in Lebanon at the time of the crime. He was released again after two days.

The prosecutor's office finally brought charges against Karim for perjury and casting false suspicion on Imad. Karim told me the story, and we decided that from now on he wasn't going to talk about it. And his brothers, as close relatives, could invoke their right to remain silent. The prosecutor's office ran out of means of proof. In the end, all that remained was a strong suspicion concerning Karim. But he had gamed it all out in advance and couldn't be charged. There were too many other possibilities; for example, Walid could have given Imad the money, or one of the other brothers could have travelled on Imad's passport—they really did all look that alike.

Naturally, they still kept smacking Karim on the back of the head, not understanding that he'd saved Walid and defeated justice.

Karim said nothing. He just thought about the hedgehog and the foxes.

Bliss

Her customer had been in politics for twenty-five years. As he undressed, he recounted how he'd worked his way up. He had put up posters, given speeches in the back rooms of little taverns, built his constituency, and won three successive rounds of voting to become a minor member of parliament. He said he had many friends and was even the head of a committee of inquiry. Naturally, it wasn't one of the major committees, but he was the head of it. He was standing in front of her in his underwear. Irina didn't know what a committee of inquiry was.

The fat man found the room too small. He was sweating. Today he had to do it in the early morning, he had a meeting at 10:00 a.m. The girl had said it was no problem. The bed looked clean, and she was pretty. She couldn't have been older than twenty, beautiful breasts, full mouth, at least five foot ten. Like most girls from Eastern Europe, she wore too much makeup. The fat man liked that. He took seventy euros from his briefcase and sat on the bed. He had laid his things carefully over the chair; it mattered to him that the creases not be messed up. The girl took off his undershorts. She pushed up the folds of fat in his stomach; all he could now see of her was her hair, and he knew she was going to need quite some time. But that's her job, he thought, and leaned back. The last thing the fat man felt was a stabbing pain in his chest; he wanted to raise his hands and tell the girl to stop, but all he could do was grunt.

Irina took the grunt to be a sign of assent, and she went on for several minutes before noticing that the man was silent. She looked up. He had turned his head to the side, saliva had run onto the pillow, and his eyes were rolled up toward the ceiling. She screamed at him, but he still didn't move. She fetched a glass of water from the kitchen and poured it on his face. The man didn't stir. He was still wearing his socks, and he was dead.

Irina had been living in Berlin for eighteen months. She would rather have stayed in her own country, where she'd gone first to kindergarten and then to school, where her family and friends lived, and where the language they spoke was her own. Irina had been a dressmaker there. She had had a pretty apartment, filled with all kinds of things: furniture, books, CDs, plants, photo albums, and a black-and-white cat that had adopted her. Her life had stretched out before her and the prospect gave her joy. She designed women's fashions; she'd already made several dresses, and even sold two of them. Her sketches were light and transparent. She dreamed of opening a little shop on the main street.

But her country was at war.

One weekend, she drove to see her brother in the country. He had taken over their parents' farm, which excused him from military service. She persuaded him to walk to the little lake that bordered the farm. They sat on the small dock in the afternoon sun while Irina told him about her plans and showed him the pad with her new designs. He was delighted and put an arm around her shoulder.

When they came back, the soldiers were standing in the farmyard. They shot her brother and raped Irina, in that order. The soldiers were in fours. One spat in her face as he lay on top of her. He called her a whore, punched her in the eyes. After that, she ceased to defend herself. When they all left, she remained lying on the kitchen table. She wrapped herself in the red-and-white tablecloth and closed her eyes, hoping it would be forever.

The next morning, she went to the lake again. She thought it would be easy to drown herself, but she couldn't do it. When she rose back up to the surface, she jerked open her mouth and her lungs filled with oxygen. She stood in the water naked; there was nothing but the trees on the bank, the reeds and the sky. She screamed. She screamed until her strength left her; she screamed against death and loneliness and pain. She knew she would survive, but she also knew that this was no longer her homeland.

A week later, they buried her brother. It was a simple grave with a wooden cross. The priest said something about guilt and forgiveness, while the mayor stared at the ground and clenched his fists. She gave the key to the farm to her next-door neighbour, along with the few remaining livestock, plus all the contents of the house. Then she picked up her little suitcase and her purse and took the bus into the capital. She did not turn around. She left the sketchbook behind.

She checked on the streets and in bars to find the names of smugglers who could get her into Germany. The agent was practised, and he took all the money she had. He knew that what she wanted was security and that she would pay for it—there were lots like Irina, and they made for good business.

Irina and the others were taken in a minibus toward the West. After two days, they stopped in a clearing, got out, and ran through the night. The man, who led them over streams and through a swamp, didn't say much, and when they had reached the end of their strength, he told them they were in Germany. Another bus brought them to Berlin. It stopped somewhere on the edge of the city. The weather was cold and foggy. Irina was exhausted, but she believed she'd reached safety.

Over the next months, she got to know other men and women from her homeland. They explained Berlin to her, its authorities and its laws. Irina needed money. She couldn't work legally; she wasn't even allowed to be in Germany. The women helped her in the first few weeks. She stood on the Kurfürstenstrasse, and she learned the price for oral and vaginal sex. Her body had become a stranger to her; she used it like a tool. She wanted to survive, even if she didn't know for what. She didn't feel herself anymore.

He sat on the footpath every day. She saw him as she got into men's cars, and she saw him in the early mornings when she went home. He had placed a plastic bowl in front of him, into which people sometimes threw money. She got used to the sight of him; he was always there. He smiled at her, and after a few weeks, she smiled back.

When winter set in, Irina took him a blanket from a secondhand shop. He was delighted. 'I'm Kalle,' he said, and let his dog sit on the blanket, wrapping him up and scratching behind his ears, while he himself stayed squatting on some newspapers. Kalle wore thin trousers; he froze even as he kept the dog warm. Irina's legs were trembling and she hurried on. She sat down on a bench around the corner, pulled up her knees, and buried her head. She was nineteen years old, and for a whole year no one had hugged her. She cried for the first time since that afternoon back home.

When his dog was run over, she was standing on the opposite footpath. She saw Kalle running across the street in slow motion and dropping to his knees in front of the car. He lifted up the dog. The driver yelled after him, but Kalle walked down the middle of the street with the dog in his arms, and he did not turn around. Irina ran after him. She understood his pain, and suddenly she knew that they were soul mates. They buried the dog together in the city park, and Irina held Kalle's hand.

That's how it all began. At some point, they decided to try to make a go of it together. Irina moved out of her filthy boardinghouse and they found a one-room apartment. They bought a washing machine and a TV, and then gradually everything else. It was Kalle's first apartment. He had run away from home at sixteen, and since then he'd been living on the street. Irina cut his hair, bought him pants, T-shirts, pullovers and two pairs of shoes. He found a job distributing brochures and helped out in the evenings at a bar.

Now men came to the house and Irina didn't have to walk the streets anymore. When they were alone again in the mornings, they got their bedding out of the cupboard, lay down, and held each other tight, lying together, naked, silent, motionless, listening only to each other's breathing, and shutting out the world. They never spoke about the past.

Irina was afraid of the dead fat man, and she was afraid of being arrested on illegal immigration charges and then deported. She decided to go to her girlfriend's and wait for Kalle there. She grabbed her purse and ran down the stairs, leaving her mobile phone forgotten on the kitchen table.

Kalle had ridden his bike with its little trailer to the industrial zone, as he did every day, but today the man who parcelled out the work said he had nothing for him. It took Kalle half an hour to get home. As he took the elevator up, he thought he heard the sound of Irina's shoes clacking on the stairs. When he unlocked the door to the apartment, she was going out the front door downstairs, on her way to the bus stop.

Kalle sat on one of the two wooden chairs and stared at the dead fat man and his blindingly white undershirt. The breakfast rolls he had brought with him were lying on the floor. It was summer, and the room was warm.

Kalle tried to concentrate. Irina would be put in prison

and then she'd have to go back to where she'd come from. Maybe the fat man had hit her—she never did things without a reason. Kalle thought about the day they had taken the train out to the country. They had lain down in a meadow in the summer heat, and Irina had looked like a child. He had been happy. Now he thought he was going to have to pay. And Kalle thought about his dog. Sometimes he went to the place in the park to see if anything had changed.

Half an hour later, Kalle knew he'd made a mistake. He had stripped down to his undershorts and now his sweat was mingling with the blood in the bathtub. He had pulled a plastic bag over the man's head because he didn't want to see his face while he was working. At first, he'd gone at it the wrong way and tried to sever the bones. Then he remembered how you dismember a chicken, and he twisted the fat man's arm out of his shoulder. Now it was going better, all he had to do was cut through the muscles and the fibrous tissue. At some point, the arm lay on the yellow tiled floor, the watch still on the wrist. Kalle turned around to the toilet bowl and threw up again. Then he ran water in the washbasin, dunked his face into it, and rinsed out his mouth. The water was cold and made his teeth ache. He stared into the mirror and didn't know whether he was standing in front of it or behind it. The man facing him had to move in order for him to do likewise. When the water overflowed the edge of the basin and splashed down onto his feet, Kalle pulled himself together. He knelt back down on the floor and picked up the saw.

Three hours later, he had detached the various limbs. He bought black garbage bags in a grocery store, attracting odd looks from the girl at the checkout counter. Kalle tried not to think about what he was going to do with the head, but he was unsuccessful. If it stays attached to the neck, I won't be able to get him into the trailer, he thought. There's no way. He left the store. Two housewives were having a conversation on the footpath, the suburban train went by, and a boy kicked an apple across the street. Kalle felt himself getting angry. 'I'm not a murderer,' he said out loud as he was passing a pram. The mother turned around and stared after him.

Back at home, he pulled himself together. One of the handles of the handsaw had come loose and Kalle cut his fingers. He burst out crying like a child; bubbles formed below his nostrils. He cried and sawed and sawed and cried, holding the fat man's head tightly under his arm. The plastic bag had become slippery and kept sliding out of his grip. When he had finally detached the head from the trunk, he was astonished to find how heavy it was. Like a sack of charcoal for a barbecue, he thought, and wondered how charcoal had popped into his mind. He'd never cooked anything on a barbecue.

He dragged the biggest bags into the elevator and used them to block the automatic door. Then he fetched the rest. The garbage bags didn't tear—he'd doubled them for the torso. He pulled the bicycle trailer into the lobby, where there was no one to see him. There were four garbage bags. The only things he'd had to put in his backpack were the arms; the trailer was full, and they would have fallen out.

Kalle had put on a clean shirt. He needed twenty minutes to reach the park. He thought about the head, about its sparse hair, and about the arms. He felt the fat man's fingers against his back. They were wet. He fell off the bike and tore off his backpack, then just dropped to the grass. He waited for people to come running and start screaming, but they didn't. Nothing happened.

Kalle lay there, looking up into the sky, and waited.

He buried the fat man in the city park in his entirety. The handle of the spade broke, so he knelt down and used the blade in his hands. He crammed everything into the hole, not a metre from the dead dog. It wasn't deep enough, so he trampled the garbage bags together. His clean shirt was filthy, his fingers black and bloody, and his skin itched. He threw the remains of the spade into a garbage container. Then he sat on a park bench for almost an hour, watching students play frisbee.

When Irina got back from her girlfriend's, the bed was empty. The fat man's jacket and folded trousers were still hanging over the chair. She clapped her hand over her mouth so as not to cry out. She understood immediately: Kalle had tried to save her. The police would find him. They would believe he'd killed the fat man. The Germans solve every murder; you keep seeing it on television, she thought. Kalle would go to prison. A mobile phone was ringing endlessly in the fat man's jacket. She had to do something.

She went into the kitchen and called the police. The men on duty could hardly understand a word she said. When they came, they looked into the bathroom and took her into custody. They asked where the body was, Irina didn't know what to reply. She kept saying the fat man had died 'normally', that it had been a 'dead heart'. The police, naturally, didn't believe her. As she was being taken out of the building, Kalle came riding up. She looked at him and shook her head. Kalle misunderstood, leapt off his bike, and ran to her. He stumbled. The police apprehended him, too. Later, he said it was fine, that he wouldn't have known what to do without Irina anyway.

Kalle remained silent. He had learned silence, and prison didn't frighten him. He had been there more than once already—break-ins, thefts. He'd heard my name inside, and asked me to take on his defence. He wanted to know what was going on with Irina; he didn't care about himself. He said he had no money but that I had to take care of his girlfriend.

I knew if Kalle would testify, he'd be saved, but he was hard to convince. All he kept asking was if that wouldn't damage Irina. He clutched at my forearms, trembled, said he didn't want to make any mistakes. I calmed him down and promised I would find a lawyer for Irina. Finally, he agreed.

He led the detectives to the hole in the city park and stood by as they dug up the fat man and sorted out the body parts. He also showed the police the place where he'd buried his dog. It was a misunderstanding. They also dug up the dog's skeleton and looked at him questioningly.

The forensic pathologist established that all the wounds had occurred after death. The fat man's heart was examined. He had died of a heart attack; there was absolutely no question about it. The suspicion of murder had been eliminated.

In the end, the only thing actionable was the dismemberment. The prosecutor considered a charge of disturbing the dead. The law states that it is forbidden to commit a 'public nuisance' with a corpse. There was no doubt, said the prosecutor, that sawing up and burying a dead body constituted a public nuisance.

The prosecutor was right. But that was not the issue. The only issue was the intention of the accused. Kalle's goal was to save Irina, not to desecrate the body. 'A public nuisance caused by love,' I said. I cited a decision of the federal court that justified Kalle's actions. The prosecutor raised his eyebrows, but he closed the file.

The arrests were nullified, and both were let go. With the help of a lawyer, Irina filed a claim for asylum and was allowed to remain in Berlin for the moment. She was not placed in a detention centre pending deportation.

They sat next to each other on the bed. The hinge on one of the cupboard doors had been broken and pulled loose during the search, and the door hung at an angle. Otherwise, nothing had changed. Irina held Kalle's hand as they looked out of the window.

'Now we have to do something new,' said Kalle. Irina nodded and thought how blissfully lucky they were.

Summertime

Consuela was thinking about her grandson's birthday: today was the day she'd have to buy the PlayStation. Her shift had started at 7:00 a.m. Working as a maid was demanding, but it was a secure job, better than most she'd had before this. The hotel paid somewhat over the going rate; it was the best in town.

All she had left to do was to clean room number 239. She entered the time on the work sheet. She was paid by the room, but the hotel management insisted that the work sheet be adhered to. And Consuela did whatever the management wanted. She couldn't lose the job. She wrote 3:26 p.m. on the work sheet.

She rang the bell. When no one opened the door, she knocked and waited some more. Then she inserted a key card into the electronic lock and pushed the door open a hand's breadth. Following the way she'd been taught, she called out,

'Maid service.' When there was no answer, she went in.

The suite occupied about thirty-five square metres and was decorated in tones of warm brown. The walls were padded with beige cloth, and there was a bright carpet on the parquet floor. The bed was rumpled and a bottle of water stood open on the nightstand. Between the two orange chaises longues was the naked body of a young woman. Consuela saw her breasts, but the head was hidden. Blood had soaked into the woollen fibres along the edge of the carpet, leaving a jagged pattern of red. Consuela held her breath. Her heart racing, she took two cautious steps forward. She had to see the woman's face. That was when she screamed. In front of her was a mushy mass of bone, hair and eyes, a portion of the whitish brain matter had sprayed out of the ruptured skull onto the dark parquet, and the heavy iron lamp that Consuela dusted every day was sticking up out of the face, covered in blood.

Abbas was relieved. He had now confessed it all. Stefanie sat next to him in her little apartment and wept.

He was a child of Palestinian refugees and had grown up in the settlement of Shatila in Beirut. His playgrounds lay between barracks with corrugated iron doors, five-storey houses pockmarked with bullet holes, and ancient cars from Europe. The children wore tracksuits and T-shirts with Western slogans on them, five-year-old girls covered their heads despite the heat, and there was warm bread wrapped in thin paper. Abbas had been born four years after the great massacre. Back then, the Christian Lebanese militia had mutilated and killed hundreds of people, women had been raped, and even children were shot. No one could arrive at an accurate count afterward, and the fear never went away again. Sometimes Abbas lay down on the clay of his unpaved street and tried to count the hopeless tangle of power lines and phone lines that were slung between the houses and carved up the sky.

His parents had paid the smugglers a great deal of money; he was supposed to have a future in Germany. He was seventeen then. Naturally, he wasn't granted asylum and the authorities gave him no permission to hold a job. He lived on state benefits; everything else was forbidden him. Abbas couldn't go to the movies or to McDonald's; he owned neither a PlayStation nor a mobile phone. He learned the language on the street. He was a pretty boy, but he had no girlfriend. And if he'd had one, he couldn't have invited her to a meal even once. All Abbas had was himself. He sat around, he spent twelve months throwing stones at pigeons, watching TV in the hostel for asylum seekers, and dawdled along the Kurfürstendamm, looking in shop windows. He was bored to death.

At some point, he began with minor break-ins. He got caught, and after the third caution by the judge in juvenile court, he underwent his first prolonged detention. It was a wonderful time. He met lots of new friends in jail, and by the time he was released, some things had become clear to him. He'd been told that for people like him—and inside there were a lot of people like him—the only way to go was drug dealing.

It was really easy. One of the bigger dealers, who didn't work the streets anymore himself, took him on. Abbas's turf was one of the subway stations, and he shared it with two other people. At first, he was only the 'bunker', a human safe-deposit box for narcotics. He kept the bags in his mouth. The other guy conducted the negotiations and the third handled the money. They called it 'work'.

The junkies asked for 'browns' or 'whites'; they paid with ten- and twenty-euro bills that they had stolen or begged or earned from prostitution. Transactions went swiftly. Sometimes women offered themselves to the dealers. If one of them was pretty enough, Abbas would take her along. To begin with, it interested him, because the girls would do anything he asked. But then he began to be disturbed by the craving in their eyes. It wasn't him they wanted; it was the drugs in his jacket.

When the police came, he had to run. He learned quickly how to recognise them; even their civilian clothes were a kind of uniform: sneakers, bum bags and hip-length jackets. And they all seemed to go to the same barber. While Abbas ran, he swallowed. If he managed to choke down the cellophane packages before they caught up with him, the proof would be hard to come by. Sometimes they administered purgatives. Then they sat next to him and waited till he threw up the little packages into a sieve. From time to time, one of his new friends would die when his stomach acids dissolved the cellophane too quickly.

As a business it was dangerous, fast and lucrative. Abbas had money now, and he sent substantial amounts home regularly. He wasn't bored anymore. The girl he was in love with was named Stefanie. He had watched her for a long time dancing in a disco. And when she turned around to him he—the big drug dealer, the king of the street—blushed.

Of course she knew nothing about his drug business. In the mornings, Abbas left love letters for her attached to the refrigerator. He told his friends that when she drank, he could see the water running down inside her throat. She became his homeland; he had nothing else. He missed his mother, his brothers and sisters, and the stars over Beirut. He thought about his father, who had slapped him merely because he had stolen an apple from the fruit stand. He'd been seven years old at the time. 'There are no criminals in our family,' his father had said. He had gone with him to the fruit seller and paid for the apple. Abbas would have liked to become an auto mechanic, or a painter, or a carpenter—or anything. But he became a drug dealer. And now he was no longer even that.

A year earlier, Abbas had gone to an arcade for the first time. At the beginning, he only went there with his friends. They pretended and acted out being James Bond and fooled around with the pretty girls who worked there. But then he went there on his own, though everyone had warned him. The poker machines were what drew him. At some point, he had started to talk to them. Each one of them had its own character, and, like gods, they determined his fate. He knew he was a compulsive gambler. He'd been losing every day for four months. He could hear the melody of the slot machines in his sleep, announcing that somebody had won. He couldn't help himself; he had to play.

His friends no longer took him along when they were dealing; he was nothing but an addict himself now, no different from their customers, the junkies. He would end up stealing money from them, they knew what his future would be, and Abbas knew they were right. But that was nowhere near the worst of it.

The worst of it was Danninger. Abbas had borrowed money from him, five thousand euros, and he had to pay back seven thousand. Danninger was a friendly man; he'd said that anyone could have a problem sometimes. Abbas hadn't felt alarmed, either. He would certainly win back the money again; the poker machines couldn't go on making him lose forever. He was wrong. On the day payment was due, Danninger had come and held out his hand. After that, things happened fast. Danninger had pulled a pair of pliers out of his pocket. Abbas saw the handles; they were covered with yellow plastic and glinted in the sun. Then the little finger of Abbas's right hand was lying on the curb. As he was screaming in pain, Danninger had handed him a handkerchief and told him the quickest way to the hospital. Danninger was still friendly, but he also said that the interest on the debt had now increased. If Abbas failed to repay ten thousand in three months' time, he'd have to cut off his thumb, then his hand, and so on until he reached his head. Danniger said he was really sorry. He liked Abbas, he was a nice guy, but there were rules, and no one could bend those rules. Abbas didn't doubt for one moment that Danninger meant it.

Stefanie cried more over the finger than over the lost money. They didn't know what to do next, but at least they were facing it together. And they would find some solution—they had found solutions for everything in the past two years. Stefanie said that Abbas needed to go into therapy immediately. But that didn't address the financial problem.

Stefanie wanted to go back to work as a waitress. With tips, that would be eighteen hundred euros a month. Abbas didn't like the idea of her working in a beer garden; he was jealous about the customers. But that was the only way they could do anything. He couldn't go back to drug dealing; they would just beat him up and throw him out.

A month later, it was clear that they wouldn't be able to pull the money together this way. Stefanie was in despair. She had to find a solution; she was afraid for Abbas. Danninger was a cipher to her, but she had rebandaged Abbas's hand every day for two weeks.

Stefanie loved Abbas. He was different from the boys she'd known before, more serious, less familiar. Abbas did her good, even if her girlfriends made stupid remarks about him. Now she was going to do something for him: she was going to save him. She even found the idea a tiny bit romantic.

Stefanie had nothing she could sell. But she knew how pretty she was. And like all her girlfriends she had read the personal ads in the newspaper and laughed over them. Now she was going to answer one of them, for Abbas and for their love.

At the first meeting with the man in the luxury hotel, she was so nervous, she shook. She was standoffish to him, but the man was friendly and not at all the way she'd imagined him. He was even nice-looking, and well groomed. Admittedly, she'd felt sick when he took hold of her and she had to service him, but she'd managed somehow. He was no different from men she'd known before Abbas, just older. Afterward, she showered for thirty minutes and brushed her teeth till her gums bled. Now there were five hundred euros in her hiding place in the coffee can.

She lay on the sofa in her apartment, bundled up in her bathrobe. She would only have to do it a few times and she'd have the money she needed. She thought about the man from the hotel, who lived in another world. The man wanted to meet her once or twice a week and pay her five hundred euros per session. She would get through it. And she was confident she would come away from it all unscathed. It was just that Abbas must know nothing about it. She would surprise him and give him the money, telling him she'd gotten it from her aunt.

Percy Boheim was tired. He looked out of the hotel window. Autumn had arrived, the wind was tearing the leaves from the trees, the days with their glowing light were over, and Berlin would soon sink back into its winter grey for at least five months. The student had gone. She was a nice girl, a little shy, but so were they all at the beginning. There was nothing ambiguous about it; it was a business transaction. He paid and got the sex he needed. No love, no phone calls in the night, no other nonsense like that. If she got too close to him, he would end it.

Boheim didn't like prostitutes. He'd tried it once years ago and it repelled him. He thought of Melanie, his wife. She was widely known as a dressage rider, and like many riders, she lived, finally, for her horses. Melanie was cold; it was a long time since they'd had anything to say to each other, but they were polite in their dealings and had reached a mutual understanding. They didn't see each other very often. He knew she would never be able to tolerate his girls. And he couldn't cope with a divorce right now, because of their son Benedict. He would have to wait another few years for the boy to grow up. Benedict loved his mother.

Percy Boheim was one of the leading industrialists in the country; he had inherited the majority shareholding in an auto-parts manufacturing company from his father, sat on the boards of many companies, and was an economic adviser to the government.

He thought about the imminent takeover of a bolt factory in Alsace. His auditors had advised against it, but they were never good judges of anything. He had long had the feeling that lawyers and auditors were good for creating problems, never solving them. Maybe he should just sell everything and go fishing. One day, thought Boheim, one day, when Benedict is old enough. Then he went to sleep.

Abbas was uneasy. Stefanie had been asking odd questions recently: did he ever think of other women? Did she still please him? Did he still love her? She had never asked things like that before. Until now she had been a little unsure of herself when they were making love, but she behaved as if she had the upper hand in their relationship; now that all seemed to have been overturned. After they'd had sex, she would nestle against him for the longest time, and even when she was asleep, she held tight to him. That was new, too.

When she had dropped off to sleep, he got up and checked her mobile phone. It wasn't the first time he'd done it.

Now there was a new entry: 'P.B.' He ran through all their acquaintances in his head; not one of them that he could think of had those initials. Then he read her stored messages. 'Wednesday 12 noon, Park Hotel. Room 239 as usual.' The text message was from P.B. Abbas went into the kitchen and sat on one of the wooden chairs. He was so enraged, he could hardly breathe. 'As usual,' so it hadn't been the first time. How could she? Now, during the biggest crisis of his life. He loved her; she was everything to him. He had thought they would get through this together. Abbas couldn't get his mind around it.

The next Wednesday at twelve noon, he was standing in front of the Park Hotel. It was the best hotel in Berlin. And that was his problem. The concierge at the front door hadn't let him in. Abbas didn't take it personally; he didn't exactly look like their regular hotel guests. He knew people's reactions to someone who looked like an Arab. So he sat down on a bench and waited. He waited for more than two hours. Finally, Stefanie came out of the hotel. He went to meet her and watched her reaction. She was shocked, and turned red.

'What are you doing here?' she asked.

'I was waiting for you.'

'How did you know I was here?' She was asking herself how much he actually knew.

'I followed you.'

'You followed me? Are you nuts? Why did you do that?'

'You have somebody else. I know it.' Abbas had tears in his eyes and was clutching her arm.

'Don't be ridiculous.' She pulled free and ran across the square, feeling like she was in a movie.

He ran two steps behind her and seized hold of her again. 'Stefanie, what did you do in the hotel?'

She had to pull herself together. Think clearly, she told herself. 'I applied for a job; they pay better than the beer garden.' It was the best she could think of.

Abbas, naturally, did not believe her. They had a loud fight on the square. She was embarrassed. Abbas yelled; she pulled him away. At some point, he calmed down. They drove back to the apartment. Abbas sat at the kitchen table, drinking tea, saying nothing.

Boheim had been meeting Stefanie for two months now. She had set aside her shyness. They got on well together, too well perhaps. Stefanie had told him that her boyfriend had followed her two weeks before. Boheim was uneasy; he knew he would have to end the arrangement. That was the dumb thing in such relationships. A jealous boyfriend spelled problems.

He arrived late today; the meeting had gone on forever. He switched on the car phone and dialled her number. It was good to hear her voice. He said he would be there in a moment. She was pleased and told him she was already naked.

He hung up as he drove into the hotel garage. He would tell her it was over. Best that it be right away, today. Boheim was not a man to procrastinate.

The file lay open on the desk. For now, there were only two folders in the customary red cardboard binders for criminal files, but this number would increase. The file displeased Assistant Prosecutor Schmied. He closed his eyes and leaned back. Only eight months till I retire, he thought. For the last twelve years, Schmied had been the head of the Capital Crimes Section in the prosecutor's office in Berlin. And now he'd had enough. His father came from Breslau; Schmied considered himself to be a Prussian through and through. He didn't hate the criminals he pursued; it was simply his duty. He didn't want another big case; he would have preferred a few straightforward murders, dramas that played themselves out within families, cases that resolved themselves speedily. But he prayed there would not be anything requiring a lot of reports he'd have to take to the prosecutor.

Schmied was looking at the request for a warrant against Boheim. He still hadn't signed it. It'll set off the whole frenzy with the press, he thought. The tabloids were already full of the naked student in the ritziest hotel. He could pretty much imagine what would happen if Percy Boheim, chairman and principal shareholder of Boheim Industries, was arrested. All hell would break loose and the spokesman for the prosecutor's office would be getting new orders by the day for what he had to say.

Schmied sighed and thought back to the note his new colleague had briefed him with. The new colleague was a good man, still a little overzealous, but that would temper itself with time. The note summarised the files in an orderly fashion.

Stefanie Becker had been found dead at 3:26 p.m. Her head had been beaten in with numerous blows of extreme force. The murder weapon was a cast-iron lamp stand, part of the standard furnishings of the room. 'Blunt-force trauma,' in the language of medical examiners.

Percy Boheim had been the last caller to the victim's mobile phone. The day after the body was discovered, two officers of the Homicide Division had visited him in his Berlin office. 'Only a couple of routine questions,' they'd said. Boheim had asked a company lawyer to join him at the meeting. The police report indicated that aside from this, he had evinced no reaction. They had shown him a photo of the deceased and he had denied knowing the girl. The phone call he explained by saying he had misdialled, and the location of his mobile phone by the fact that he'd driven past the hotel. The policemen wrote up his statement right there in the office; he read it through and signed it.

At this point, it was already clear that the conversation had lasted almost a minute, far too long to be a wrong number. Nonetheless, the police had not pointed this out to Boheim. Not yet. They had also not yet revealed that his number was stored in the deceased's phone memory. Boheim had made himself suspicious.

The next day, the analysis of the trace evidence came in: sperm had been found in the hair and on the breasts of the deceased. The DNA had not been on file in the data bank. Boheim had been asked to give a sample of his saliva voluntarily. His DNA was analysed immediately—it matched the sperm. That, in a nutshell, was the report.

The yellow folder with the autopsy photographs was, as always, distasteful to Schmied. He went through it only briefly: pitiless images against a blue background, the sight of them bearable only if deliberately contemplated for a very long time.

Schmied thought of the many hours he'd spent in autopsy. Everything happened quietly there, just the sound of scalpels and saws, the voices of the doctors murmuring their shorthand into dictating machines as they handled the bodies with respect. Jokes around the autopsy table happened only in thrillers. The only thing he would never get used to was the smell, that typical odour of decay—almost every pathologist felt the same way. Nor was it possible to smear some Vicks under your nose, as certain trace evidence could only be deduced from the smell of the corpse. As a young prosecutor, Schmied had been sickened when the blood was ladled out of the bodies and weighed or when the organs were placed back in the body after the postmortem. Later he had come to understand that there was a specific art in sewing the corpse back up after autopsy firmly enough to prevent it from leaking, and he had realised that medical examiners had serious conversations about it. It was a parallel universe, just as his was. Schmied and the chief medical examiner were friends, they were almost the same age, and they never discussed their professional lives in private.

Assistant Prosecutor Schmied sighed a second time, then signed the order of arrest and took it to the examining magistrate. Only two hours later, the judge issued the warrant, and six hours later, Boheim was arrested in his apartment. Simultaneously, searches were initiated in the couple's various apartments, offices and houses in Düsseldorf, Munich, Berlin, and Sylt. The police had organised it well.

Three lawyers appeared for the arraignment, looking like alien beings in the examining magistrate's little office. They were civil lawyers, highly paid specialists in corporate takeovers and international arbitration. None of them had appeared before a judge; the last time they'd been engaged with criminal law was when they were studying for their law degrees. They didn't know what motions they should file, and one of them said threateningly that he might have to bring politics into this. The judge remained calm nonetheless.

Melanie Boheim sat on the wooden bench outside the door to the hearing room. No one had told her she couldn't see her husband—the arraignment was not open to the public. On the advice of his lawyers, Boheim said nothing when the warrant was read. The lawyers had come with a blank cheque and certification from the bank that he was good for up to fifty million euros. The examining magistrate was angered by the figure; it reeked of the class system. He refused bail—'We're not in America here'—and asked the lawyers if they wished to apply for a formal review of the remand in custody.

Assistant Prosecutor Schmied had said almost nothing during the hearing. This was going to be a fight, and he thought he could hear the starting bell.

Percy Boheim was impressive. The day after his arrest, I went to find him in the house of detention where he was being held, after having been asked by the chief counsel of his firm to take over the defence. Boheim sat behind the table in the visitor's cell as if it were his office, and greeted me warmly. We talked about the government's failed tax policies and the future of the car industry. He behaved as though we were at a stand-up reception and not preparing for a jury trial. When we got around to the actual matter at hand, he said immediately that he had lied to the police when they had questioned him, in the hopes of protecting his wife and saving his marriage. To all my other questions, his answers were precise, focused, and devoid of hesitation.

Of course he had known Stefanie Becker. She had been his lover; he had got to know her via an ad in one of the Berlin papers. He had paid her for sex. She was a nice girl, a student. He had thought about offering her a place as a trainee in one of his companies once she'd graduated. He had never asked her why she was working as a prostitute, but he was certain he had been her only customer; she was shy and it was only over time that she thawed out. 'It all sounds ugly now, but it was what it was,' he said. He'd liked her.

On the day it happened, he'd had a meeting that ran until 1:20 and had reached the hotel somewhere around 1:45. Stefanie was waiting; they'd had sex. After that, he'd showered and then left immediately, because he wanted to have some time alone to prepare for his next appointment. Stefanie had stayed in the room in order to take a bath before she set off, and she had told him she didn't want to be out of there until 3:30. He had tucked five hundred euros in her purse, which was their standard arrangement.

He had used the elevator next to the suite to go down directly to the underground garage; it would have taken him a minute, two at most, to get to his car. He had left the hotel at around 2:30 and driven to the zoological garden, Berlin's biggest park, and taken a walk for the better part of an hour, thinking in part about his relationship with Stefanie and deciding that he had to end it. He'd left his mobile phone switched off; he hadn't wanted to be disturbed.

At four o'clock, he'd been at a meeting on the Kurfürstendamm with four other men. Between 2:30 and 4:00, he had met no one, nor had he had any phone conversations. And no one had passed him when he left the hotel.

Defendants and defence lawyers have a curious relationship. A lawyer doesn't always want to know what actually happened. This also has its roots in our code of criminal procedure: if the defence counsel knows that his client has killed someone in Berlin, he may not ask for 'defence witnesses' to take the stand who would say that the man had been in Munich that day. It's a tightrope walk. In other cases, the lawyer absolutely has to know the truth. Knowledge of the actual circumstances may be the tiny advantage that can protect his client from a guilty verdict. Whether the lawyer thinks his client is innocent is irrelevant. His task is to defend the accused, no more, no less.

If Boheim's explanation was correct—that is, that he'd left the room at 2:30 and the cleaning lady had found the girl's body at 3:26, then there was a little under an hour to deal with. It was enough. In the space of sixty minutes, the real perpetrator could have entered the room, killed the girl, and disappeared before the cleaning lady entered. There was no proof of what Boheim had told me. If he had kept silent during his first interview, it would have been easier. His lies had made the situation worse, and there was absolutely no trace of another attacker. Admittedly, I did think it unlikely that a jury would end up convicting him in a major trial. But I doubted that any judge would withdraw his arrest warrant right now—a suspicion clung.

Forty-eight hours later, the examining magistrate called me to arrange a time for the formal review of Boheim's remand in custody. We settled on the next day. I could have the file picked up by a courier; the prosecutor's office had approved its release.

The file contained new inquiries. Everyone in the victim's mobile-phone address book had been questioned. A girl-friend, in whom Stefanie Becker had confided, explained to the police why she had turned to prostitution.

But what was much more interesting was that the police had located Abbas in the meantime. He had a record—break-ins and drug dealing and, two years previously, an offence involving grievous bodily harm, a fight outside a discotheque. The police had questioned Abbas. He said he had followed Stefanie to the hotel once, out of jealousy, but she'd been able to explain what she was doing there. The interrogation went on for many pages, and the detectives' suspicions were clear in every line. But finally when it came down to it, they had a motive but no proof.

Late in the afternoon, I paid a visit to Assistant Prosecutor Schmied in his office. As always, he welcomed me in both a friendly and a professional way. He didn't feel good about Abbas, either. Jealousy was always a powerful motive. Abbas could not be excluded as the alternative killer. He knew the hotel, she was his girlfriend, and she had slept with another man. If he had been there, he could also have killed her. I explained to Schmied why Boheim had lied, then said, 'Sleeping with a student isn't, finally, a crime.'

'Yes, but it's not very attractive, either.'

'Thank god that's not the issue,' I said. 'Infidelity is no longer punishable under the law.' Schmied himself had had an affair with a female prosecutor some years ago, as everyone knew around the Moabit courthouse. 'I can't see a single reason why Boheim would have wanted to kill his lover,' I said.

'Nor do I, yet. But you know motives don't count that much with me,' said Schmied. 'He really did lie his head off under questioning.'

'That makes him suspicious, I grant you, but it doesn't prove anything. Besides which, his first statement at the hearing is probably unusable.'

'Oh?'

'The police had already analysed the phone records by then. They knew he'd had long conversations with the victim. They knew from the nearest mobile-phone tower that his car was in the neighbourhood of the hotel. They knew he had reserved the room in which the girl was killed. The police should therefore have interrogated him formally as the accused, but they only questioned him under the guise of a witness and only cautioned him as such.'

Schmied thumbed through the transcript of the interrogation. 'You're right,' he said finally, and pushed the files away. He disliked such little games by the police; they never really got anybody anywhere.

'Besides which, the weapon involved, the lamp the student

was killed with, showed no fingerprints,' I said. The trace evidence had revealed only *her* DNA.

'That is correct. But the sperm in the girl's hair came from your client.'

'Oh come on, Mr Schmied, that's just crazy. He ejaculates on the girl and then pulls on his gloves to bash her head in? Boheim's not a moron.'

Schmied's eyebrows shot up.

'And all the other traces, the ones that were lifted off water glasses, door handles, window handles, and so on, are perfectly explicable by the fact that he stayed in the hotel—they imply no guilt.'

We argued for almost an hour. At the end, Schmied said, 'On condition that your client lays out his relationship to the deceased in detail at the hearing, I will agree that the arrest warrant may be withdrawn tomorrow morning.'

He stood up and held out his hand to say goodbye. As I was standing in the doorway, he said, 'But Boheim will surrender his passport, pay a high amount in bail, and check in with the police twice a week. Agreed?'

Of course I agreed.

When I left the room, Schmied was pleased that the affair would now die down. He had never really believed Boheim to be the perpetrator. Percy Boheim gave no appearance of being a raving madman who would crush the head of a student with a rain of blows. But, Schmied was also thinking, who knows his fellow human being? Which was why, for him, motive was very seldom the deciding factor.

Two hours later, just as he was locking the door to his office on his way home, his phone rang. Schmied cursed, went back, picked up the receiver, and let himself down into his chair again. It was the Homicide Division's leading investigator on the case. When Schmied hung up six minutes later, he looked at the clock. Then he pulled his old fountain pen out of his jacket, wrote a brief summary of the conversation, and inserted it as the first page on top of the file, switched off the light, and remained sitting for some time in the darkness. He now knew that Percy Boheim was the killer.

The next day, Schmied asked me to come to his office again. He looked almost sad as he pushed the pictures at me across his desk. The photos clearly showed Boheim behind his car window. 'There's a high-resolution camera positioned at the exit from the hotel garage,' he said. 'Your client was filmed leaving that garage. I received the pictures this morning— the Homicide Division called me last night after you and I had spoken. I wasn't able to reach you again.'

I looked at him, puzzled.

'The pictures show Mr Boheim leaving the hotel garage. Please look at the time on the first photograph; the video camera always stamps them in the bottom left-hand corner. The time is shown as 3:26:55. We checked the clock setting on the camera; it's correct. The cleaning lady discovered the dead girl at 3:26. That time is also correct; it's confirmed by the first call to the police, which came in at 3:29. I'm sorry, but there can't be any other perpetrator.'

I had no alternative but to withdraw from the remand

hearing. Boheim would remain in detention as a suspect until the trial.

The next months were taken up with preparations for the trial. All the lawyers in my chambers were working on it; every tiny detail from the file was checked and rechecked—the mobile-phone tower, the DNA analysis, the camera in the garage. The Homicide Division had done good work; there were almost no mistakes we could find. Boheim Industries commissioned a private detective agency, but it came up with nothing new. Boheim himself stuck to his story, despite all proof to the contrary. And despite his miserable prospects, he remained good-humoured and relaxed.

Police work proceeds on the assumption that there is no such thing as chance. Investigations consist 95 percent of office work, checking out factual details, writing summaries, getting statements from witnesses. In detective novels, the person who did it confesses when he or she is screamed at; in real life, it's not that simple. And when a man with a bloody knife in his hand is bent over a corpse, that means he's the murderer. No reasonable policeman would believe he had only walked past by chance and tried to help by pulling the knife out of the body. The detective superintendent's observation that a particular solution is too simple is a screenwriter's conceit. The opposite is true. What is obvious is what is plausible. And most often, it's also what's right.

Lawyers, by contrast, try to find holes in the structures of proof built by prosecutors. Their ally is chance; their task is to disrupt an overhasty reliance on what appears to be the truth.

A police officer once said to a federal judge that defence lawyers are no more than brakes on the vehicle of justice. The judge replied that a vehicle without brakes isn't much use, either. Any criminal case can function only within these parameters. So we were hunting for the chance that would save our client.

Boheim had to spend Christmas and New Year's in detention. Assistant Prosecutor Schmied had given him wide-ranging permission for conversations with his operating officers, accountants and civil lawyers. He saw them every second day and ran his companies out of his detention cell. His board members and his staff declared openly that he had their support. His wife also visited him regularly. The only person he refused to be visited by was his son; he didn't want Benedict to see his father in prison.

But still there was no ray of hope that broke through for the trial, due to start in four days. Aside from a few procedural motions, no one had a basic concept for a successful defence. A deal, otherwise a regular occurrence in criminal cases, was out of the question. Murder carries a life sentence, manslaughter a sentence of five to fifteen years. I had nothing that would allow me to negotiate with the judge.

The printouts of the video pictures were on the library table in my chambers. Boheim had been captured on them in piercing detail. It was like a pocket camera strip with six images. Boheim activates the exit button with his left hand. The barrier opens. The car drives past the camera. And then suddenly it was all completely clear. The solution had been in the file for four months, so simple that it made me laugh. And we'd all overlooked it.

The trial took place in Room 500 in the courthouse in Moabit. The state's case was for manslaughter. Assistant Prosecutor Schmied represented the prosecutor's office himself, and as he read out the charges, the courtroom fell silent. Boheim took the stand as the accused. He was well prepared; he spoke for more than an hour without notes. His voice was sympathetic; people liked listening to him. He spoke with great focus about his relationship with Stefanie Becker. He left nothing out; there were no dark, shadowy areas. He described the course of their meeting on the day of the crime and how he had left the hotel at 2:30. He answered the relevant questions from the judges and the prosecutors both fully and precisely. He explained both that he had paid Stefanie Becker for sex and why, adding that it would be absurd to assume that he would have killed a young girl with whom he had had no deeper relationship.

Boheim was masterful. The discomfort of everyone involved in the trial was evident. It was a strange situation. No one wanted to suspect him of murder—it was just that it couldn't have been anyone else. Witnesses were not due to be called until the next day.

The tabloids the following morning led with such headlines as MILLIONAIRE NOT KILLER OF BEAUTIFUL STUDENT? That was one way of summing it up.

On the second day of the trial, they called Consuela, the hotel maid. Finding the body had taken its toll on her. Her statements about the time were credible. Neither the prosecution nor the defence had any questions for her.

After her, it was Abbas's turn. He was in mourning. The court asked about his relationship to the deceased, in particular whether Stefanie had ever spoken about the accused and, if so, what she had said. Abbas had nothing he could report.

Then the presiding judge asked Abbas about his meeting with Stefanie in front of the hotel, his jealousy, and his spying on her. The judge was fair; he did everything to ascertain if Abbas had been in the hotel on the day of the murder. Abbas responded no to every question in this vein. He described his gambling obsession and his debts, said he had recovered now and had a limited work permit, which enabled him to wash dishes in a pizzeria to clear those debts. No one in the court believed Abbas was lying: anyone willing to lay bare his private circumstances in such a way would be telling the truth.

Assistant Prosecutor Schmied also tried everything. But Abbas stuck to his story. He was on the witness stand for almost four hours.

I didn't have any questions for Abbas. The presiding judge looked at me in surprise; after all, Abbas was the only potential alternative killer. I had something else in mind.

Famously, the most important rule for a defence counsel when examining a witness is never to ask a question to which you do not already know the answer. Surprises are not always happy ones, and you do not play with the fate of your client.

The trial produced almost nothing new; the contents of the files were laid out step by step. Stefanie's girlfriend, to whom she had admitted why she had turned to prostitution, merely cast a shadow on Boheim, who had taken advantage of the girl's plight. One of the female jurors, who seemed to me to be on our side, shifted uneasily on her chair.

On the fourth day of the trial, the policeman we'd been waiting for was called as the twelfth witness. He hadn't been part of the Homicide Division for very long. It had been his job to secure the video from the surveillance camera in the garage. The presiding judge asked how the policemen had handled the video's transfer from the security team at the hotel. Yes, he had immediately checked the time coded on the video on the monitors in the hotel's security office. He had been able to establish that there was a mere thirty-second deviation from the actual time. And he had written this up in his report.

When the defence was invited to cross-examine, I first asked him to confirm that the date he had secured the video was October 29. Yes, that was correct. It was a Monday, around 5:00 p.m.

'Sir, did you ask the watchman at the hotel whether he moved the clocks back to winter time on October twenty-eighth?' I asked.

'Excuse me? No. The time stamp was correct, I checked it…'

'The video was taken on October twenty-sixth, which still falls within summer time. The changeover to winter time only occurred two days later, on October twenty-eighth.'

'I don't understand,' said the policeman.

'It's quite simple. It could be that the clock setting inside the surveillance camera was showing winter time. If this clock registered three o'clock in summer, it would actually be two o'clock, but if it were winter, three o'clock would be the correct time.'

'Right.'

'On the day of the murder, October twenty-sixth, it was still summer time. The clock showed three-twenty-six. If the clock hadn't been reset, it would actually have been two-twenty-six. Do you understand?'

'Yes,' said the policeman, 'but that's all very theoretical.'

'The theory is the point. The question is whether the clock was correctly set. If not, then the accused left the room an hour before the maid discovered the body. This hour would have allowed any other person to kill the victim. That, sir, is why it would have been critical to ask the hotel's security staff this question. Why did you not ask it?'

'I can't remember if I asked or not. Probably the security people told me...'

'I have here a statement from the head of the security team that we obtained some days ago. He said the clock had never been reset. Ever since the camera was installed, it has run on the same time, which is winter time. Could you now try to better recall whether you asked him this question or not?' I handed the presiding judge and the prosecutor's staff a copy of the statement.

'I...I think I didn't pose that question,' the policeman now said.

'Your Honour, would you please show the witness sheets twelve to fifteen from picture folder B? It concerns the pictures that show the accused leaving the garage.'

The presiding judge found the yellow picture folder and spread out the prints from the video camera in front of him. The witness stepped over to the judges' table and looked at them.

'There it is: three twenty-six fifty-five—that's the time,' said the policeman.

'Yes, the wrong time. May I direct your attention to the accused's arm as it appears in image number four? Please look carefully. His left hand is clearly visible because he's pressing the buzzer. Mr Boheim was wearing a Patek Philippe that day. Can you make out the numerals in the picture?'

'Yes, they're perfectly legible.'

'Sir, what time are they telling?'

'Two twenty-six,' said the policeman.

Unrest broke out on the jammed press bench. Assistant Prosecutor Schmied now approached the judges' table himself to look at the original pictures. He took his time, picked up the photos one by one, and inspected them closely. Finally, he nodded. That gave us the sixty minutes needed to present the theory of an alternative killer and free Boheim. The rest of the trial would be over quickly now; there were no other pieces of evidence against Boheim. The presiding judge declared a recess.

Half an hour later, the prosecutor's office lifted the order of detention on Boheim, and at next day's proceedings, he was formally exonerated without any further evidence being heard.

Assistant Prosecutor Schmied congratulated Boheim on the verdict. Then he went back down the long hall to his office, finished a summary report on the outcome of the trial, and opened the next file that was lying on his desk. Three months later, he retired.

Abbas was arrested that same evening. The police interrogator was skilful. He explained to Abbas that Stefanie had only prostituted herself to save him, and read him the statement from the girlfriend to whom Stefanie had told the whole story. When Abbas understood the sacrifice she'd made, he broke down. But he had had experience with the police, and he didn't confess—the crime remains unsolved to this day. Abbas could not be accused of it; the evidence was insufficient.

Melanie Boheim instituted divorce proceedings four weeks after the end of the trial.

Schmied didn't cotton onto the whole time business until some months later, after he'd retired. It was a mild autumn day and he just shook his head. It wouldn't justify a retrial, nor would it explain the time as shown on Boheim's watch. He kicked a chestnut out of the way and walked slowly down the allée, thinking how strange life was.

Self-Defence

Lenzberger and Beck were ambling along the platform. Shaved heads, military pants, Doc Martens, big strides. Beck's jacket said THOR STEINAR; Lenzberger's T-shirt said PITBULL GERMANY.

Beck was somewhat shorter than Lenzberger. Eleven convictions for assault, his first when he was fourteen and went along with the big guys, joining in when they kicked a Vietnamese to a pulp. It only got worse from there. He was fifteen when he did his first stretch in juvie; at sixteen, he got himself tattooed. Above the knuckle on each finger of his right hand was a letter of the alphabet; taken together they read H-A-T-E; on his left thumb he had a swastika.

Lenzberger had only four convictions on his sheet, but he had a new metal baseball bat. In Berlin, they sell fifteen times more baseball bats than balls.

Beck started by picking on an old lady, who became

frightened. He laughed and took two big strides toward her with his arms held high. The lady's little steps grew quicker; she clutched her purse against her chest and vanished.

Lenzberger swung the bat against a rubbish bin. The reverberation rang through the station; he didn't need much strength to put a dent in the metal. The platform was almost empty, the next train, an intercity express to Hamburg, would not be leaving for forty-eight minutes. They sat down on a bench. Beck put his feet up; Lenzberger squatted on the armrest. Bored, they threw the last beer bottle down onto the tracks. It broke, and the label peeled off slowly.

That was when they discovered him. The man was sitting two benches away. Mid-forties, bald on top, the rest of his head surrounded by a fringe of hair, glasses with standard-issue black frames, grey suit. A bookkeeper or a clerk, they thought, some bore with a wife and children waiting for him back home. Beck and Lenzberger grinned at each other: a perfect victim, easily frightened. It hadn't been a good night so far, no women, not enough money for really good stuff. Beck's girlfriend had split up with him on Friday; she'd had enough of the brawling and the booze. Life this Monday morning was shit—until they came across the man. Their fantasies running to violence, they clapped each other on the shoulder, linked arms, and went up to him. Beck sat down with a thump on the bench next to him and burped in his ear, releasing a stench of alcohol and undigested food. 'Hey, old man, had a fuck today?'

The man pulled an apple out of his pocket and polished it on his sleeve.

'Hey, arsehole, I'm talking to you,' said Beck. He hit the

apple out of the man's hand and crushed it underfoot so that flesh spurted over his Doc Martens.

The man didn't look at Beck. He stayed sitting, motionless, looking down. Beck and Lenzberger took this as a provocation. Beck jabbed his forefinger into the man's shirt. 'Oh, someone doesn't want to talk,' he said, and hit the man over the ear. The glasses slipped down, but the man didn't push them back into place. He still hadn't moved, so Beck pulled a knife out of his boot. It was a long knife, the tip sharpened on both sides and the back serrated. He brandished it in front of the man's face, but the man's eyes didn't move. Beck stabbed it a little into the man's hand, nothing deep, a pinprick. He looked at the man expectantly as a drop of blood welled up on the back of his hand. Lenzberger was enjoying the idea of what would come next and swung the baseball bat against the bench in his excitement. Beck stuck a finger into the blood and smeared it around. 'Well, arsehole, feeling better?'

The man still didn't react. Beck lost his temper. The knife sliced through the air twice from right to left, a mere fraction of an inch from the man's chest. The third time, it made contact, slashing his shirt and making an eight-inch gash in his skin, almost horizontally, which bled into the material and left a thickening red streak.

A doctor who was intending to take the early train to Hannover to a conference of urologists was standing on the platform opposite. He would testify later that the man barely moved; it all happened so fast. The CCTV camera on the platform recorded the incident, showing only individual images in black and white.

Beck swung again and Lenzberger whooped. The man gripped the hand holding the knife and simultaneously struck the crook of Beck's arm. The blow altered the direction of the knife without interrupting the swing itself. The blade described an arc as the man aimed the tip between Beck's third and fourth ribs. Beck stabbed himself in the chest. As the steel penetrated the skin, the man struck Beck's fist hard. It was all one single motion, fluid, almost a dance. The blade disappeared completely into Beck's body and pierced his heart. Beck lived for another forty seconds. He stood there, looking down at himself, clutching the knife handle, and seemed to be reading the tattoos on his fingers. He felt no pain; the nerve synapses were no longer transmitting any signals. Beck didn't realise he was in the process of dying.

The man rose, turned toward Lenzberger, and looked at him. His body language didn't convey any message; he just stood there and waited. Lenzberger didn't know whether to fight or flee, and because the man still looked like a book-keeper, he made the wrong decision. He swung the baseball bat high in the air. The man hit him only once, a brief chop to Lenzberger's neck that happened so fast the CCTV camera couldn't capture it on the individual frames. Then he sat down again without casting another glance at his opponent.

The blow was precise, hitting the carotid sinus, which is a brief surface dilation of the internal carotid artery. This tiny location contains a whole bundle of nerve endings, which registered the blow as an extreme increase in blood pressure and sent signals to Lenzberger's cerebrum to reduce his heartbeat. His heart slowed and slowed, and his circulation did likewise. Lenzberger sank to his knees; the baseball bat landed on the ground behind him, bounced a couple of times, rolled across the platform, and fell onto the train tracks. The blow had been so hard that it had torn the delicate wall of the carotid sinus. Blood rushed in and overstimulated the nerves. They were now transmitting a constant signal to inhibit the heartbeat. Lenzberger collapsed facedown on the platform; a little blood trickled into the ridged tiles and pooled against a cigarette pack. Lenzberger died: his heart had simply stopped beating.

Beck remained standing for another two seconds. Then he, too, fell; his head banged against the bench and left a smear of red. He lay there, eyes open, seeming to be looking at the man's shoes. The man straightened his glasses, crossed his legs, lit a cigarette, and waited to be arrested.

A policewoman was the first to arrive. She and a colleague had been dispatched when the two skinheads went onto the platform. She saw the bodies, the knife in Beck's chest, the man's slashed shirt, and she registered that he was smoking. All information being processed in her brain with equal importance, she pulled out her gun, aimed it at the man, and yelled, 'Smoking is forbidden everywhere in the station.'

'A key client has asked for our help. Please take the case and we will be responsible for the costs,' said the lawyer when he called. He said he was calling from New York, but it sounded as if he was there right next to me. He was making it urgent. He was the senior partner in one of those corporate law firms that have at least one branch in every industrialised country.

A 'key client' is one who produces a large stream of business for the law firm, hence a client with very special rights. I asked him what it was about, but he didn't know anything. His secretary had received a phone call from the police; all she'd been told was that someone had been arrested at the station. She didn't get a name. It definitely involved 'manslaughter or something', but that was all she knew. It had to be a 'key client', because they were the only ones who were ever given that number.

I drove to the Homicide Division in the Keithstrasse. It makes no difference whether police stations are in modern high rises built of glass and steel or in two-hundred-year-old guardhouses—they're all alike. There is grey-green linoleum in the corridors, the air smells of detergents, and there are oversize posters of cats in all the interrogation rooms, along with postcards that colleagues have sent from their holidays. Clippings with jokes are stuck to computer screens and cupboard doors. There is lukewarm filtered coffee from orange-yellow coffee machines with scorched warming plates. On the desks there are heavy I LOVE HERTHA mugs, green plastic pencil holders, and sometimes there are photos of sunsets on the walls in glass holders without frames, taken by some clerk. The décor is practical and light grey, the rooms are too cramped, the chairs are too ergonomic, and on the windowsills are plastic-looking plants in self-irrigating pebble trays.

Head of Homicide Dalger had conducted hundreds of interrogations. When he had arrived at Homicide sixteen years earlier, it was the leading division in the whole police structure. He was proud to have made it, and he knew that he owed his successful rise to one quality above all others: patience. When necessary, he listened for hours on end; nothing was too much for him, and even after all the long years in the police, he still found everything interesting. Dalger avoided interrogations right after an arrest, when everything was still fresh and he didn't know very much. He was the man for confessions. He didn't use tricks, he didn't use blackmail, and he didn't use humiliation. Dalger was glad to leave the first interrogation to his juniors; he didn't want to start asking questions until he felt he knew everything there was to know about the case. He had a brilliant memory for details. He didn't rely on instinct, even when that instinct had never let him down in the past. Dalger knew that the most absurd stories can be true and the most believable stories false. 'Interrogations,' he told his juniors, 'are hard work.' And he never forgot to finish by saying, 'Follow the money or follow the sperm. Every murder comes down to one or the other.'

Although we almost always had conflicting interests, we respected each other. And when I had finally talked my way through to him and entered the interrogation room, he seemed almost delighted to see me. 'We're not getting anywhere here,' was the first thing he said. Dalger wanted to know who had retained me. I gave him the name of the law firm. Dalger shrugged his shoulders. I asked everyone to leave the room so that I could speak to my client undisturbed. Dalger grinned. 'Good luck.'

The man didn't look up until we were alone. I introduced myself; he nodded politely but didn't say anything. I tried it in German, English, and rather bad French. He just looked at me and didn't utter a word. When I set out a pen for him, he pushed it back toward me. He didn't *want* to talk. I put a power of attorney form in front of him; somehow, I had to be able to document that I had the authority to represent him. He seemed to be thinking, and then suddenly he did something strange: He opened an ink pad that was on the table and pressed his right thumb first into the blue colour and then onto the space for the signature on the power of attorney. 'That's another possibility,' I said, and collected the form. I went into Dalger's office, and he asked me who the man was. This time, I was the one to shrug my shoulders. Then he gave me a thorough rundown of what had happened.

Dalger had taken custody of the man the day before from the federal police, who were responsible for the station. The man hadn't uttered a single syllable either when arrested or while he was being transported, or during the first attempted interrogation in the Keithstrasse. They had tried with different interpreters; they had read him his rights before the interrogation in sixteen languages—nothing.

Dalger had ordered the man to be searched, but they found nothing. He had no briefcase, no passport, and no keys. He showed me the so-called Search Protocol, Part B, which listed the objects that had been found. There were seven:

1. Tempo brand tissues with a price tag from the station pharmacy.
2. Cigarette packet with six cigarettes, German customs sticker.
3. Plastic lighter, yellow.
4. Second-class ticket to the central station in Hamburg

(no seat reservation).

5. 16,540 euros in notes.
6. 3.62 euros in coins.
7. A card from the legal firm of Loruis, Metcalf and Partners, Berlin, with a direct-dial phone number on it.

The most striking thing, however, was that his clothes had no labels—the trousers, jacket and shirt could have come from a tailor, but there aren't many people who have their own socks and undershorts custom-made. Only his shoes gave evidence of origin; they came from Heschung, a shoemaker in Alsace—and it was possible to buy them in good shops outside France, as well.

The man was processed by the police Records Department. He was photographed and fingerprinted. Dalger also ran this information through all the databases. There was no match; the man was unknown to the investigating authorities. Not even the origin of the ticket gave them anything; it had come from an automatic dispenser in the station.

In the meantime, the videotape from the station had been viewed, and the doctor on the opposite platform and the frightened old lady interviewed. The police had worked with utter thoroughness and utter lack of success.

The man had been arrested and spent the night at the police station. The next day, Dalger had dialled the number on the card. He had waited as long as he could before doing this. Lawyers never make things simple, he thought.

We sat in Dalger's room, drinking lukewarm filtered coffee. I watched the videotape twice and said to Dalger that it was self-evidently a virtual textbook case of self-defence.

Dalger didn't want to release the man: 'Something about him doesn't add up.'

'Yes, of course that's obvious. But apart from this instinct of yours, you know you have no grounds to hold him,' I replied.

'We still don't know anything, not even his identity.'

'No, Herr Dalger, that's not anything; it's the *one* thing you don't know.'

Dalger made a call to prosecutor Kesting. It was a so-called Cap-One, which is to say a legal proceeding that fell within the Capital Crimes parameters of the prosecutor's office. Kesting was already familiar with the case from Dalger's first report. He was at a loss, but resolute: a quality that is sometimes effective in the prosecutor's office. Which is why he decided to have the man appear before the examining magistrate. A few telephone calls later, we were given instructions to be there at five that afternoon.

The examining magistrate's name was Lambrecht, and he was wearing a Norwegian sweater, although it was springtime. He suffered from low blood pressure, had felt cold his whole life, which was also why he was in an almost permanent bad temper. He was fifty-two years old, and he wanted clarity; things had to be orderly and he didn't want to take any demons home with him from the office.

Lambrecht was a guest lecturer in trial law at the high school, and because of the real-life examples he used, his lectures had become legendary. He told the students it was a mistake to believe that judges enjoyed convicting people. 'They do it when it is their duty, but they don't do it when they have doubts.' The real meaning of judicial independence was that judges, too, wanted to be able to sleep at night. That was the point at which the students always laughed. Nonetheless, it was the truth; he had come across almost no exceptions.

The job of examining magistrate is perhaps the most interesting in the criminal justice system. You get a brief look into everything, you don't have to put up with boring, long trials, and you aren't obliged to listen to anyone else. But that is only one side of it. The other is the loneliness. The examining magistrate reaches his decisions alone. Everything depends on him: he sends a man to prison or sets him free. There are simpler ways of earning a living.

Lambrecht wasn't exactly thrilled by defence lawyers. But then he wasn't exactly thrilled by prosecutors, either. What interested him was the case, and he reached decisions that were hard to predict in advance. Most people complained about him; his massively oversized glasses and his pale lips gave him a strange look, but he commanded universal respect. At the celebration for his twentieth year on the job, he received a certificate from the president of the district court. The president asked him if he still enjoyed what he did after so many years. Lambrecht's response was that he'd never enjoyed it. He was an independent man.

Lambrecht read the witnesses's statements, and after he, too, failed to get the man to speak, he said he wanted to see the video. We had to watch it with him around a hundred times in succession. I could draw each frame by then; it went on for an eternity.

'Switch the thing off,' he finally said to the sergeant, and turned to face us. 'Now, gentlemen, I'm listening.'

Kesting, naturally, had already provided the request for an arrest warrant, without which there would have been no meeting. He was applying for the man's arrest for two instances of manslaughter, and stating that the man was a flight risk, as he had no provable identity. Kesting said, 'It is certainly plausible that this was a situation involving self-defence. But excessive force was used.'

The prosecutor's office was therefore going for a charge of so-called excessive self-defence. When you are attacked, you have the right to defend yourself, and there is no limit to your choice of means. You may respond to a fist with a cudgel, and to a knife with a gun; you are under no obligation to choose the mildest form of counterattack. But equally, you may not overreact: if you've already rendered your attacker helpless with a pistol shot, you may not cut off his head for good measure. The law does not tolerate such excesses.

'The excess was constituted by the man striking the knife that was already embedded in the victim's chest,' said Kesting.

'Aha,' said Lambrecht. He sounded astonished. 'And now defence counsel, please.'

'We all know this is madness,' I said. 'Nobody is obliged to tolerate an assault with a knife, and of course he was allowed to defend himself in his fashion. And the prosecutor's office is certainly not occupied with these questions. Prosecutor Kesting is far too experienced to believe he could bring any such charge before a jury. He simply wants to establish the man's identity, and needs the time to do so.'

'Is this so, Mr Prosecutor?' asked Lambrecht.

'No,' said Kesting. 'The prosecutor's office does not file frivolous requests for arrest warrants.'

'Aha,' said the judge again. This time, it sounded ironic. He turned toward me. 'And can you tell us who the man is?'

'Herr Lambrecht, you know I may do no such thing, even if I were able. But I can provide a viable address.' I had had another telephone conversation in the meantime with the lawyer who had engaged me. 'The man can be summoned via a lawyer's office, and I can verbally guarantee the lawyer's agreement.' I handed over the address.

'You see!' exclaimed Kesting. 'He declines to speak out. He knows much more, but he declines to speak out.'

'These legal proceedings are not against me,' I said. 'But this is how we find ourselves: we do not know why the accused declines to speak. It's possible he doesn't understand our language. But it's also possible that he's declining to speak for some other—'

'He's contravening paragraph one eleven of the law,' Kesting interrupted. 'It is absolutely clear he's contravening it.'

'Gentlemen, I would be grateful if you would take turns speaking,' said Lambrecht. 'Paragraph one eleven states that every defendant must provide his or her particulars. In this, I agree with the prosecutor's office.' Lambrecht was taking off his glasses, putting them on again, taking them off again. 'But this, of course, in no way constitutes a rule that justifies an order of arrest. Twelve hours are the limit during which a person may be detained simply for purposes of establishing the particulars of an identity. And these twelve hours, Mr Prosecutor, have already long expired.'

'Besides which,' I said, 'the accused is not always invariably obliged to provide all his particulars. If his truthful statements might expose him to the risk of criminal prosecution, he is allowed to remain silent. If the man were to say who he is, and if this were to lead to his arrest, then of course he has the right to remain silent.'

'There you have it,' said Kesting to the examining magistrate. 'He will not tell us who he is, and there's nothing we can do.'

'That's how it is,' I said. 'There's nothing you can do.'

The man sat on the bench, radiating indifference. He was wearing a shirt with my initials on it; I'd had it sent over to him. It fitted him, but it looked odd.

'Mr Prosecutor,' said Lambrecht, 'is there any prior relationship between the accused and the victims?'

'No, we have no such information,' said Kesting.

'Were the victims drunk?' Lambrecht was correct in this line of thought, too; in any situation involving self-defence, a drunk is to be avoided.

'Point zero four and point zero five blood-alcohol levels respectively.'

'That's insufficient,' said Lambrecht. 'Have you found out anything about the perpetrator that is not yet in the files? Is there any evidence of another crime or another arrest warrant?' Lambrecht seemed to be ticking off a list.

'No,' said Kesting, knowing that every 'no' was putting him further and further from his goal.

'Are there any ongoing inquiries?'

'Yes. The complete autopsy report has not yet been delivered.' Kesting was happy he had turned up something he could cite.

'Yes, well, the two of them are unlikely to have died of

heatstroke, Herr Kesting.' Lambrecht's voice now softened, a bad sign for the prosecutor's office. 'If the prosecutor has nothing more to produce than what I have here on my table, I will now render my decision.'

Kesting shook his head.

'Gentlemen,' said Lambrecht, 'I have heard enough.' He leaned back. 'The issue of self-defence is more than clear. If someone is threatened with a knife and a baseball bat, if he's stabbed and swung at, he is allowed to defend himself. He is allowed to defend himself in such a way that the attack is definitively ended, and the accused did no more than that.'

Lambrecht paused for a moment, then went on: 'I agree with the prosecutor that the case seems unusual. I can only say that I find the calm with which the accused faced the victims frightening. But I cannot recognise where the claim of excessive force resides. The correctness of this conclusion is also demonstrated by the fact that I would certainly have granted an order of arrest against the two attackers if they were in front of me now instead of lying on the pathologist's table.'

Kesting clapped his files shut. The noise was too loud.

Lambrecht dictated into the records, 'The prosecutor's request for an arrest warrant is hereby denied. The accused is to be released forthwith.' Then he turned to Kesting and me. 'That's all. Have a good evening.'

While the court recorder was preparing the release form, I went outside. Dalger was sitting on the visitor's bench, waiting.

'Good evening. What are you doing here?' I asked. It's unusual for a policeman to show such interest in the outcome of a legal proceeding.

'Is he out?'

'Yes. It was a clear case of self-defence.'

Dalger shook his head. 'Thought so,' he said. He was a good policeman who hadn't had any sleep for the last twenty-six hours. The business was obviously annoying him, and this was, obviously, equally unusual for him.

'What's up?'

'Well, you don't know about the other thing.'

'What other thing?'

'The same morning your client was taken into custody, we found a dead body in Wilmersdorf. Stabbed in the heart. No fingerprints, no traces of DNA, no fibres, nothing. Everyone associated with the dead man has an alibi, and the seventy-two hours are running out.'

The seventy-two-hour rule states that the chances of solving a murder or manslaughter start to decline rapidly after seventy-two hours.

'What are you trying to say?'

'It was a professional job.'

'Stab wounds to the heart are not infrequent,' I said.

'Yes and no. At least they're not this precise. Most people need to stab more than once, or the knife gets stuck in the ribs. It usually goes wrong.'

'And?'

'I have this feeling...your client...'

Naturally, it was more than a feeling. Every year, around 2,400 fatal crimes are recorded in Germany, approximately 140 of them in Berlin. That's more than in Frankfurt, Hamburg and Cologne combined, but even with an annual success rate of 95 percent, that leaves seven cases a year in which the perpetrator is never caught. And here a man had just been released who fitted perfectly into Dalger's theory.

'Herr Dalger, your feeling—' I began, but he didn't let me finish.

'Yes, yes, I know,' he said, and turned away. I called after him that he should phone me if there were any new developments. Dalger muttered something incomprehensible, along the lines of 'no cause…lawyers…always the same…' and went home.

The man was released straight from the hearing room, he collected his money and the other objects, and I signed for him. We walked to my car and I drove him to the same station where he had killed two men thirty-five hours earlier. He got out without saying a word and disappeared into the crowd. I never saw him again.

A week later, I had a lunch date with the head of the corporate law firm. 'So who is your key client who wanted an unknown man looked after?' I asked.

'I'm not permitted to tell you; you would know him. And I myself don't know who the unknown man is. But I have something for you,' he said, and pulled out a bag. It held the shirt I'd given the man. It had been cleaned and ironed.

On the way to the parking lot I threw it in the garbage.

Green

They had brought a sheep again. The four men stood around the animal in their rubber boots and stared at it. They had driven it into the courtyard of the manor house in the bed of a pickup truck, and now it was lying there in the drizzle on a sheet of blue plastic. The sheep's throat had been cut and its mud-stained fleece was dotted with stab wounds. The crusted blood was gradually dissolving again in the rain, running across the plastic in thin red threads until it seeped away among the paving stones.

Death was no stranger to any of the men; they were livestock farmers, and every one of them had slaughtered animals before. But this dead body was giving them the shivers: the sheep was a Bleu-du-Maine, a vigorous breed with a bluish head and prominent eyes. The animal's eyeballs had been gouged out and the rims of the dark eye sockets showed the frayed remains of the optic nerves and cords of muscle.

Count Nordeck greeted the men with a nod; nobody was in the mood to talk. He glanced briefly at the animal, shaking his head, then pulled a wallet out of his jacket pocket, counted out four hundred euros, and gave the money to one of the men. It was more than double what the sheep was worth. One of the farmers, capturing what every one of them was thinking, said, 'This can't go on.' As the men drove away from the yard, Nordeck turned up his coat collar. The farmers are right, he thought. I have to speak to him.

Angelika Petersson was a fat, contented woman. She had been the policewoman in Nordeck for twenty-two years, there had never been a killing in her district in all that time, and she had never needed to draw her gun in the course of duty. Work was over for the day, and she'd completed the report on the drunk driver. She rocked her chair back and forth, enjoying the prospect of the weekend, despite the rain. She would finally get around to sticking the photos from her last holiday into the album.

When the bell rang, Petersson groaned. She pressed the buzzer; no one came through the door, so she got to her feet with a sigh and a curse and went out onto the street. She wanted to give an earful to the village boys who still thought this idiotic game of ringing bells was funny.

Petersson almost didn't recognise Philipp von Nordeck standing on the footpath outside the guardhouse. It was pouring. Thick strands of wet hair hung down into his face, and his jacket was dripping mud and blood. He was holding the kitchen knife so tightly that his knucklebones stood out white. Water was running over the blade.

Philipp was nineteen, and Petersson had known him since he was a child. She walked up to him slowly, speaking to him soothingly and quietly, the way she had once talked to the horses on her father's farm. She took the knife out of his hand and stroked his head; he made no protest. Then she put an arm around his shoulders, led him up the two shallow stone steps into the little building, and took him to the washroom.

'Just get yourself cleaned up; you look awful,' she said. She was no forensic detective, and she just felt sorry for Philipp.

He let the hot water run and run over his hands until they turned red and the mirror fogged up. Then he bent over and washed his face; blood and dirt sluiced into the washbasin and clogged the drain. He stared into the basin and whispered, 'Eighteen.' Petersson didn't understand him. She took him into the little guardroom where she had her desk. The air smelled of tea and floor polish.

'Now please tell me what happened,' said Petersson as she sat him down in the visitor's chair. Philipp laid his forehead against the edge of her desk, closed his eyes, and said nothing.

'You know what, we're going to call your father.'

Nordeck came at once, but the only thing Philipp said was 'Eighteen. It was an eighteen.'

Petersson explained to the father that she would have to notify the local prosecutor's office, as she didn't know if something bad had happened, and Philipp wasn't saying anything that made sense.

Nordeck nodded. 'Of course,' he said, and thought, Here we go.

The prosecutor mobilised two detectives from the nearest town. When they arrived, Petersson and Nordeck were drinking tea in the office. Philipp was sitting by the window, looking out, totally cut off.

The detectives gave him the usual formal notice that he was being taken into custody, then left him under Petersson's charge. They wanted to go to the manor house with Nordeck to search Philipp's room. Nordeck showed them the two rooms on the second floor that the boy occupied. While one of the policemen was taking a look around, Nordeck stood with the other in the entrance hall. The walls were hung with hundreds of antlers of native animals, and trophies from Africa. It was cold.

The policeman stood before the enormous stuffed head of a black buffalo from East Africa. Nordeck was trying to explain the thing with the sheep. 'This is how it is,' he said, searching for the right words. 'In the last few months, Philipp has killed some sheep. Well, he slit their throats. The farmers caught him at it once and told me about it.'

'Ah, slit their throats,' said the policeman. 'These buffalo weigh more than one tonne, don't they?'

'Yes, they're pretty dangerous. A lion doesn't stand a chance against a full-grown specimen.'

'So, the boy slaughtered sheep, yes?' The detective could hardly tear himself away from the buffalo.

Nordeck took this to be a good sign. 'Of course I paid compensation for the sheep, and we also wanted to have Philipp begin…But somehow we were hoping it would all blow over. We were wrong.' Better leave out the details about the stab wounds and the eyes, thought Nordeck.

'Why does he do it?'

'I don't know. I have no idea.'

'Sounds odd, no?'

'Yes, it's odd. We have to do something with him,' Nordeck said again.

'Looks that way. Do you know what happened today?'

'What do you mean?'

'Well, was it another sheep?' asked the detective. He simply couldn't leave the buffalo alone, and had put his hands on the horns.

'Yes, one of the farmers called my mobile phone a little while ago. He's found another.'

The policeman nodded absentmindedly. He was annoyed at having to spend his Friday evening with a sheep killer, but the buffalo wasn't bad at all. He asked Nordeck if he could go to police headquarters in town on Monday to give a brief statement. He'd had enough of paperwork and wanted to get home.

'Of course,' said Nordeck.

The second detective came down the stairs holding an old cigar box with VILLIGER KIEL on it in brownish-yellow lettering.

'We have to impound this box,' he said.

Nordeck realised that the policeman's voice had suddenly taken on an official tone. Even the latex gloves he was wearing somehow conveyed a new formality. 'If you think so,' said Nordeck. 'What's in there? Philipp doesn't even smoke.'

'I found this box behind a loose tile in the bathroom,' said the policeman. Nordeck was angered by the very idea that there were loose tiles in the house at all. The policeman cautiously opened the box. His colleague and Nordeck leaned forward, then immediately recoiled.

The box was lined with plastic and divided into two compartments. An eyeball, somewhat compressed and still a little wet, stared out of each compartment. A photograph of a girl was glued to the inside of the lid—Nordeck recognised her immediately: it was Sabine, the daughter of Gerike, the primary school teacher. She had celebrated her sixteenth birthday the previous day. Philipp had been there, and he had often talked about her before. Nordeck had assumed his son had fallen in love with her. But now he blanched: the girl in the picture had no eyes—they'd been cut out.

Nordeck, hands trembling, hunted for the teacher's phone number in his address book. He held the receiver so that the policemen could listen in. Gerike was surprised by the phone call. No, Sabine was not at home. She had gone on directly after the birthday party to visit a friend in Munich. No, she hadn't yet checked in, but that was nothing unusual.

Gerike tried to calm Nordeck: 'Everything's okay. Philipp took her to the night train.'

The police questioned two employees at the train station, they turned Nordeck's house upside down, and they interviewed everyone who'd been at the birthday party. It all produced nothing about where Sabine might actually be.

The pathologist examined the eyes in the cigar box. They were sheep's eyes. And the blood on Philipp's clothing was animal blood.

A few hours after Philipp's arrest, a farmer found another

sheep behind his farmyard. He loaded it onto his shoulders and carried it down the village street in the rain all the way to the police station. The animal's fleece was saturated; it was heavy. Blood and water streamed down over the farmer's waxed jacket. He threw the carcass down onto the steps of the station house; the wet fleece smacked against the door and left a dark stain on the wood.

Halfway between the manor house and the village, which consisted of roughly two hundred low houses, a narrow path branched off and led to the abandoned reed-thatched Friesian house on the dike. By day, it was the focal point of children's games; by night, couples met under the pergola. You could hear the sea from here, and the crying of the gulls.

The detectives found Sabine's mobile phone in the wet beach grass, and, not far from it, a hair band. Sabine had been wearing it the evening of her birthday, her father said. The area was sealed off and a hundred policemen combed the marshland with their bloodhounds. Forensic investigators in their white overalls were summoned and did a search for further evidence, but they found nothing more.

The army of policemen also attracted the press to Nordeck, and anyone who set foot on the street was interviewed. Almost no one left the house, curtains stayed closed, and even the village tavern remained empty. Only the journalists with their garish computer bags filled the tables in the bar, laptops open, cursing the slow internet connection and stringing one another along with invented pieces of news.

It had been raining uninterrupted for days, at night the mist pressed down heavily on the roofs of the low houses, and even the cattle seemed to be morose. The villagers talked about it all, and they no longer greeted Nordeck when they saw him.

On the fifth day after Philipp's arrest, the media liaison in the prosecutor's office issued a photograph of Sabine to the newspapers, along with an appeal for information as to her whereabouts. The next day, someone smeared the word *murderer* in red on the wooden gate to the manor house.

Philipp was in jail. For the first three days, he said almost nothing, and the few words he did utter were incomprehensible. On the fourth day, he pulled himself together. The police took his statement; he was open and answered their questions. It was only when they tried to talk about the sheep that he hung his head and fell silent. Naturally, the detectives were more interested in Sabine, but Philipp kept repeating his explanation that he'd taken her to the train station. Before that, they'd gone to the house on the dike and talked. 'Like friends,' he said. Maybe that was when she'd mislaid her mobile phone and the hair band. He had done nothing to her. There was nothing more to be pried out of him. And he didn't want to speak to the psychiatrist.

Prosecutor Krauther led the interrogations. He slept so badly in the course of those days that his wife told him at breakfast he was grinding his teeth at night. His problem was that nothing had apparently gone on prior to this. Philipp von Nordeck had killed some sheep, but that was no more than property damage, technically speaking, and an offence against animal-protection laws. There had been no claim for financial damages, the sheep had been paid for by his father,

GREEN

and none of the farmers had filed charges. Sabine had not, indeed, arrived at her friend's in Munich. 'But she's a young girl, and the fact that she hasn't been heard from could be for any number of innocent reasons,' Krauther said to his wife. The cigar box was no proof, in and of itself, that Philipp had murdered the girl, even if the examining magistrate had accepted the premise of the prosecutor's application for an arrest warrant thus far. Krauther felt uneasy.

Because there weren't many cases out here in the country that raised these sorts of questions, Philipp's medical examination at least had gone quickly. No results indicating brain malfunction, no disease of the central nervous system, and no anomalies of the chromosomes. But, thought Krauther, he is, of course, absolutely insane.

When I had my first meeting with the prosecutor, it was six days after the arrest, and the review of his remand in custody was due the next day. Krauther looked tired, but he seemed pleased to be able to share his thoughts with somebody. 'Aberrant behaviour,' he said, 'has a tendency to escalate rather rapidly. If his victims have thus far been limited to sheep, couldn't they now be people?'

Wilfred Rasch established a reputation unchallenged in his lifetime as the doyen of forensic psychiatry. The view that aberrant behaviour intensifies over time is one of his scientific theories. But from everything we knew thus far about Philipp's acts, it struck me as unlikely that we were dealing with such an aberration.

Before my conversation with Krauther, I had talked to the veterinarian who, on orders from Nordeck, had destroyed the animals' remains. The police had had better things to do than interview this man, or perhaps quite simply nobody had thought to do so. The vet was a meticulous observer, and the incidents had struck him as so bizarre that he had written a short report on every dead sheep. I gave his notes to the prosecutor, who made a rapid survey. Each sheep gave evidence of eighteen stab wounds. Krauther looked at me. The policemen had also mentioned that Philipp had uttered nothing but the word *eighteen*. So it might have to do with the number itself in some way.

I said I did not think Philipp exhibited deviant sexual behaviour. The pathologist had examined the last sheep, but had found no evidence that Philipp had been sexually aroused by the killing of the animals. There was no sperm and no sign that he had penetrated the sheep.

'I don't believe Philipp suffers from perversities,' I said.

'So then what?'

'He may very well be schizophrenic,' I said.

'Schizophrenic?'

'Yes, there's something that's terrifying him.'

'That may be. But he won't talk to the psychiatrist,' said Krauther.

'Nor is he obliged to,' I replied. 'It's very simple, Herr Krauther. You have nothing. You have no corpse and you have no proof of any crime. You don't even have evidence that might point toward it. You had Philipp von Nordeck locked up because he killed sheep. But the arrest warrant was issued for the killing of Sabine Gerike. Nonsense. The only reason he's in custody is because you sort of have a bad feeling about things.'

Krauther knew I was right. And I knew that he knew.

Sometimes it's easier to be a defence lawyer than a prosecutor. My task was to be partisan and to stand in front of my clients. Krauther had to remain neutral. And he couldn't. 'If only the girl would show up again,' he said. Krauther was sitting with his back to the window. The rain hit the glass and slicked down it in broad streams. He turned in his office chair and followed my eyes to the outdoors and the grey sky. We sat there for almost five minutes, looking at the rain, and neither of us said a word.

I spent the night at the Nordecks'; the last time I'd been there was nineteen years ago for Philipp's christening. During dinner, a windowpane was shattered by a flying stone. Nordeck said it was the fifth time this week, so what was the point of calling the police. But he thought maybe I should get my car and drive it into one of the barns on the farm; otherwise, my tyres would be slashed by morning.

As I was lying in bed sometime around midnight, Philipp's sister Victoria came into the room. She was five, and her pyjamas were very jazzy. 'Can you bring Philipp home?' she asked. I got up, lifted her onto my shoulders, and took her back to her bedroom. The lintels were high enough to avoid any risk of her bumping her head, one of the few advantages of an old house. I sat down on her bed and pulled the covers up around her.

'Have you ever had a cold?' I asked her.

'Yes.'

'Well, Philipp's got something like a cold in his head. He's not so well and he needs to get better.'

'How does he sneeze in his head?' she asked. My example obviously was a bit problematic.

'You can't sneeze in your head. Philipp's just all muddled up. Maybe the same way you are when you've had a bad dream.'

'But when I wake up, everything comes right again.'

'Exactly. Philipp needs to wake up properly.'

'Are you going to bring him back here?'

'I don't know,' I said. 'I'm going to try.'

'Nadine said Philipp did something bad.'

'Who's Nadine?'

'Nadine's my best friend.'

'Philipp isn't bad, Victoria. You need to go to sleep now.'

Victoria didn't want to go to sleep. She wasn't happy that I knew so little, and she was worried about her brother. Then she asked me to tell her a story. I invented one that had no sheep in it and nobody who was sick. When she'd gone to sleep, I fetched my files and my laptop and worked in her room until the morning. She woke up twice, sat up for a moment, looked at me, and then went back to sleep again. At about 6:00 a.m., I borrowed one of the pairs of rubber boots standing in the hall and went out into the yard to smoke a cigarette. The air was raw, I was bleary-eyed from lack of sleep, and there were only eight hours until the custody hearing.

The day brought no news of Sabine, either. She'd now been missing for a week. Prosecutor Krauther was filing for an extension.

Most custody hearings are a grim business. The law requires that there be an investigation of whether there is a compelling reason to believe that the person being held in custody has committed a crime. This sounds clear and unambiguous, but is hard to grapple with in reality. At this point, the interviews of witnesses have barely begun, the legal proceedings are just starting, and there is no general overview. The judge may not make things simple for himself; he has to decide about the incarceration of someone who may not be guilty at all. Custody hearings are much less formal than trials, the public is not admitted, judges, prosecutors and defence lawyers don't wear robes, and in practice it's a serious conversation about the questions surrounding the prolonging of detention.

The examining magistrate in the case against Philipp von Nordeck was a young man who had just finished his probationary period. He was nervous and didn't want to make any mistakes. After half an hour, he said he'd heard the arguments and his decision would be issued departmentally—that is, he wanted to use the fourteen-day grace period to await further evidence. It was unsatisfying all round.

When I left the court, the rain was still coming down in buckets.

Sabine was sitting on a wooden bench on the lower deck of the ferry between Kollund and Flensburg. She had spent a happy, if wet, week with Lars at the seaside resort, which had almost nothing to offer except its beach and a furniture store. Lars was a young construction worker who had the name of his football club tattooed on his back. Sabine had kept the week with him a secret from her parents; her father didn't like Lars. Her parents trusted her, and anyway, she doubted they would call her on their own account.

Lars had accompanied her to the boat, and now Sabine was afraid. From the moment she'd boarded the little ferry, the man with the threadbare jacket had been staring at her. He was still looking right at her face, and now he was coming over to where she was. She was about to stand up and move away when the man said, 'Are you Sabine Gerike?'

'Um, yes.'

'For god's sake, girl, call home at once. They're looking for you everywhere. Take a look at the newspaper.'

Shortly after this, the phone rang in Sabine's parents' house, and half an hour later Prosecutor Krauther called me. He said Sabine had simply run off with her boyfriend and was expected back that afternoon. Philipp would be released, but he must be placed in psychiatric care. I had just agreed on this with Philipp and his father anyway. Krauther made me promise formally that I would take care of this.

I collected Philipp from the detention centre, which looked like a little jail in a children's book. Philipp, of course, was overjoyed to be free and to know that Sabine was fine. On the way back to his parents' house, I asked him if he'd like to go for a walk. We stopped by a path across the fields. The cloudy sky above us was enormous, the rain had stopped, and you could hear the harsh cries of the gulls. We talked about his boarding school, his love of motorbikes, and the music he was listening to right now. Suddenly, out

GREEN

of nowhere, he said what he hadn't wanted to say to the psychiatrist: 'I see people and animals as numbers.'

'How do you mean?'

'When I see an animal, it has a number. For example, the cow over there is a thirty-six. The gull's a twenty-two. The judge was a fifty-one, and the prosecutor a twenty-three.'

'Do you think about this?'

'No, I see it. I see it right away. The same way other people see faces. I don't ever think about it; it's just there.'

'And do I have a number?'

'Yes, five. A good number.' We both had to laugh. It was the first time since he'd been arrested. We walked on silently side by side.

'Philipp, what is it with eighteen?'

He looked at me, startled. 'Why eighteen?'

'You said it to the policewoman, and you killed the sheep with eighteen stab wounds.'

'No, that's not right. I killed them first and then I stabbed them six times in each side and then six times in the back. I had to take the eyes out, too. It was hard, the first few times they came apart.' Philipp began to tremble. Then he blurted out, 'I'm afraid of eighteen. It's the devil. Three times six. Eighteen. Do you get it?'

I glanced at him questioningly.

'The apocalypse. The Antichrist. It's the number of the beast and the number of the devil.' He was almost screaming.

The number 666 is indeed in the Bible; it appears in the Revelation of Saint John: 'Here is wisdom. Let him that hath understanding count the number of the beast: for it is the number of a man; and his number is six hundred threescore

139

and six.' It was a popular belief that with these words the Evangelist was alluding to the devil.

'If I don't kill the sheep, the eyes will consume the land with fire. The apples of the eye are sin itself; they are the apples from the tree of knowledge, and they will destroy everything.' Philipp began to cry with a child's lack of all restraint, shaking from head to foot.

'Philipp, please listen to me. You're afraid of the sheep and their terrible eyes. I can understand that. But the whole thing with the Revelation of Saint John is absolutely cuckoo. John didn't mean the devil when he used the number six sixty-six; it was a hidden play on the name of Nero, the Roman Caesar.'

'What?'

'If you add up the numbers in the Hebrew spelling of Caesar Nero, you get six sixty-six. That's all. Saint John couldn't write that out; he had to say it in numbers. It has nothing to do with the Antichrist.'

Philipp kept crying. There was no point in telling him that there's nowhere in the Bible that talks about an apple tree in paradise. Philipp was living in his own world. At a certain point, he began to calm down, and we walked back to the car. The air had been washed clean and tasted of salt. 'I have one last question,' I said after a while.

'And?'

'What does all this have to do with Sabine? Why did you do that with her eyes?'

'A few days before her birthday, I saw her eyes in my room,' said Philipp. 'They'd become sheep's eyes. And that's when I understood. I told her that evening of her birthday in the house on the dike, but she didn't want to hear it. She got frightened.'

'What was it that you understood?' I asked.

'Her first name and her last name each have six letters.'

'Did you want to kill her?'

Philipp looked at me for a long time. Then he said, 'No, I don't want to kill anyone.'

A week later, I took Philipp to a psychiatric clinic in Switzerland. He didn't want his father to go with us. After we'd unpacked his suitcase, we were welcomed by the head of the hospital, who showed us around the bright and airy modern buildings. Philipp was in a good place, insofar as you can say that about any mental hospital.

I had had lengthy phone conversations with the chief of medicine. He, too, even at long distance, had agreed that everything pointed to a case of paranoid schizophrenia. It is not an infrequent disorder; the evidence suggests that approximately 1 percent of the population will be afflicted with it once in their lives. It often manifests itself in phases that lead to the disruption of thought processes and perceptions, distorting both their form and content. Most patients hear voices; many believe they're being pursued, that they're responsible for catastrophes of nature, or they're tortured, like Philipp, by mad ideas. The treatment involves both drugs and extensive psychotherapy. Patients need to be able to trust, and to open themselves up. The odds of a full recovery are around 30 percent.

At the end of the tour, Philipp came with me to the main

door. He was just a lonely, sad, anxious boy. He said, 'You never asked what number I am.'

'That's true. And what number are you?'

'Green,' he said, and he turned on his heel and went back into the clinic.

The Thorn

Feldmayer had already had many jobs in his life. He'd been a mailman, a waiter, a photographer, a pizza maker and, for six months, a blacksmith. When he was thirty-five, he applied for a post as guard in the local museum of antiquities and got it, greatly to his astonishment.

After he'd filled out all the forms, answered the questions, and provided photographs for his building pass, he went to the uniform store, where he was handed out three grey uniforms, six medium-blue shirts, and two pairs of black shoes. A future colleague led him through the building, showed him the canteen and the rest rooms, and explained how to use the time clock. At the end, he was shown the room he would be guarding.

While Feldmayer was going through the museum, Frau Truckau, one of the two employees in HR, organised his documents, sent some of them to Accounts, and started a file.

The names of the guards were put on little cards and sorted into a file-card box. Every six weeks, the staff was shuffled in different combinations to another of the town's museums, to make the work more varied.

Frau Truckau thought about her boyfriend. Yesterday, in the café where they'd been meeting for almost eight months after work, he'd asked her to marry him. He'd turned red and stuttered. His hands had been damp; they'd left outlines on the little marble table. She had leapt to her feet with joy, kissed him in front of everyone, and then they'd run to his apartment. Now she was dead tired and bursting with plans; she would be seeing him again very soon; he'd promised to pick her up from work. She spent half an hour on the toilet, sharpened pencils, sorted paper clips, dawdled around in the hall, until finally she'd made it. She threw on her jacket, ran down the stairs to the exit, and fell into his arms. But she'd forgotten to close the window.

When the cleaning lady opened the door to the office later, a gust of wind seized the half-completed file card, which was blown to the floor and then swept up. The next day, Frau Truckau was thinking about everything imaginable, except for Feldmayer's file card. His name did not become part of the staff-rotation system, and when Frau Truckau went on maternity leave a year later because of her baby, he'd been forgotten.

Feldmayer never complained.

The hall was almost empty, eight metres high and roughly one hundred and fifty square metres. The walls and vaulted ceiling were built of brick, their red tempered to a warm glow by a coat of lime wash. The floor was made of grey-blue marble. It was at the end of a run of twelve interconnecting rooms in one wing of the museum. A bust stood in the centre of the hall, mounted on a grey stone plinth. The chair stood under the middle one of the three tall windows, and the window seat to the left held a machine that measured the humidity. It had a glass cover and ticked gently. Outside the window was an inner courtyard with a solitary chestnut tree. The next guard was installed four rooms farther along; sometimes Feldmayer could hear the distant squeaking of his rubber-soled shoes on the stone floor. Otherwise, all was silent. Feldmayer sat down and waited.

In the first weeks, he was restless, stood up every five minutes, walked around his hall, counted every step he took, and was happy to see each visitor. Feldmayer looked for things to do. He measured his hall, his only assistance a wooden ruler he'd brought from home. First, he measured the length and width of one of the marble floor slabs, then used that to calculate the size of the floor. Then he realised he'd forgotten the cracks, so he measured these as well and added them to the total. The walls and ceiling were harder, but Feldmayer had plenty of time. He kept a school notebook, in which he entered every measurement. He measured the doors and their frames, the size of the keyholes, the length of the handles, the skirting boards, the radiator covers, the window catches, the distance between the double glazing, the circumference of the humidity machine, and the light switches. He knew how many cubic metres of air there were in the hall, and how far and to which marble slab the sun's rays penetrated on every day of the year; he knew the average humidity level and its variations in the morning, at midday, and in the evening. He noted that the fifth crack between the marble slabs, counting from the door, was half a millimetre narrower than the others. The second window catch to the left had a dash of blue on the underside, something he couldn't explain, for there was nothing blue in the hall. The painter had missed a spot on the radiator cover, and there were pin-sized holes in the bricks on the back wall.

Feldmayer counted the visitors and noted how long they spent in his hall, which side they chose to view the statue from, how often they looked out of the window, who gave him a nod. He assembled statistics about male versus female visitors, about children, about classes and their teachers, about the colours of jackets, shirts, coats, pullovers, trousers, skirts and stockings. He counted how often anyone breathed in his hall, and registered how often which marble slabs got stepped on, and how often which words got spoken the most. There was one statistic for hair colour, another for eye colour, another for skin colour, yet another for shawls, for purses, for belts, and one for bald spots, for beards, and for wedding rings. He counted the flies and tried to evolve a system to account for their flight patterns and landing spots.

The museum changed Feldmayer. It began when he found himself unable to tolerate the sound of his TV in the evenings. He let it run on mute for another six months, then stopped turning it on at all, then finally gave it to the young student couple who had moved into the apartment across the hall. The next thing was the pictures. He had a few art prints, *Apples on a Cloth*, *Sunflowers* and *The Alps*. At some point, the colours began to irritate him; he took the pictures off the wall and put them in the trash. He gradually emptied his apartment: illustrated magazines, vases, decorated ashtrays, coasters, a lilac bedspread, and two plates with motifs from Toledo. Feldmayer threw them all away. He stripped the wallpaper, spackled the walls smooth and whitewashed them, got rid of the carpet, and polished the floorboards.

After a few years, Feldmayer's life had an absolutely set rhythm. He got up every morning at 6:00 a.m. Then, regardless of the weather, he walked through the municipal garden in a circle that required precisely 5,400 steps. He moved unhurriedly and knew exactly when the traffic light at the street crossing would switch to green. If ever he failed to keep to this rhythm, the rest of his day felt wrong.

Every evening, he put on a pair of old trousers and got down on his knees to polish the floorboards in his apartment—a demanding job that took almost an hour and calmed him. He did the housework with care and slept a deep, quiet sleep. On Sunday, he always went to the same local restaurant, where he ordered a grilled chicken and had two beers. Mostly, he talked to the owner, with whom he'd been at school.

Before the museum, Feldmayer had always had girl-friends, but then they began to interest him less and less. They were simply 'too much', as he said to the restaurant's owner. 'They're loud and they ask things I don't have answers to, and I can't tell them about my work.'

Feldmayer's only hobby was photography. He owned

a beautiful Leica, which he'd bought secondhand at a very good price; in one of his jobs, he'd learned to develop his own films. He'd set up a darkroom in the storage closet of his apartment, but after years in the museum, he couldn't think of any possible subjects.

He phoned his mother regularly and visited her every three weeks. When she died, he had no relatives anymore. He had his phone disconnected.

His life flowed along quietly, and he avoided any form of excitement. He was neither happy nor unhappy—just content with his life.

Until he got involved with the sculpture.

It was the thorn puller, one of the motifs of classical art. A naked boy sits on a boulder, leaning forward, his left leg bent and resting on his right thigh. With his left hand, he holds his left instep as his right hand pulls a thorn out of the sole of his foot. The marble figure in Feldmayer's hall was a Roman copy of the Greek original. It wasn't particularly valuable; there were countless such copies.

Feldmayer had measured the figure long ago, had read everything about it he could find, and would even have been able to draw from memory the shadow it cast on the floor. But sometime between his seventh and eighth year at the museum, he couldn't remember exactly anymore. That was when the trouble began. Feldmayer was sitting in his chair looking at the statue without really seeing it, when he suddenly asked himself if the boy had in fact found the thorn in his foot. He didn't know where the question came from; it was just there, and it wouldn't go away.

He went over to the figure and examined it. He couldn't find the thorn in the foot. Feldmayer became nervous, a feeling he hadn't had in years. The longer he looked, the less clear it seemed to him that the naked boy had actually managed to get hold of the thorn. That night Feldmayer slept badly. The next morning, he skipped the circuit of the municipal garden and spilled his coffee. He arrived at the museum too early and had to wait half an hour for the staff entrance to open. There was a magnifying glass in his pocket. He all but ran to his hall, then used the magnifying glass to examine the statue millimetre by millimetre. He found no thorn, either between the boy's thumb and forefinger or in his foot. Feldmayer wondered if maybe the boy had dropped it. He crawled around the statue on his knees, searching the floor. Then he felt sick and he went to the toilet and threw up.

Feldmayer wished he'd never discovered the problem with the thorn.

In the following weeks, things went downhill. He sat in the hall every day with the boy and brooded. He imagined the boy playing, maybe hide-and-seek or football. Then Feldmayer, having read about this, thought, 'No, it must have been a footrace. They were always having those in Greece. And the boy had felt a tiny prickle, which hurt, and he'd no longer been able to put weight on that foot. The others had run way ahead, but he'd had to sit down on the boulder. And the damn invisible thorn had now been sticking in his foot for hundreds and hundreds of years and was refusing to be pulled out'. Feldmayer got more and more upset. After a few months, he was having anxiety attacks as soon as he woke up.

In the mornings, he kept wandering around in the staff room and (this was the man his colleagues called 'the monk' behind his back) spent time in the canteen gossiping with anyone around, doing whatever he could to postpone his arrival in his hall until the very last minute. When he was finally there with the boy, he couldn't look at him.

It got worse. Feldmayer had sweating attacks, suffered palpitations, and started biting his fingernails. He could hardly get to sleep; when he nodded off, he had nightmares, from which he awoke soaking wet. His everyday life was no more than a shell. Soon he began to believe that the thorn was inside his head and still growing. It was scraping against the inner surface of his skull; Feldmayer could *hear* it. Everything in his life that had been empty, calm and ordered until now was transformed into a chaos of pointed barbs. And there was no way out. He had lost all sense of smell; and was having trouble breathing. Sometimes he got so little air that he did what was absolutely forbidden and pulled open one of the windows in the hall. He ate only the tiniest amounts, because he believed the food was going to choke him. He convinced himself that the boy's foot had become infected, and when he stole a glance now and then, he was sure the boy was growing bigger by the day. He had to set him free; he had to release him from the pain. Which is how Feldmayer came upon the idea of the drawing pins.

In an office-supply shop, he bought a box of drawing pins with strikingly harsh yellow heads. He bought the smallest ones he could find; he didn't want the pain to be too great.

There was a shoe shop three streets farther on. Feldmayer didn't have to wait long: a scrawny man tried on a shoe, cried out in pain, hopped over to a bench on one leg, cursing, and pulled a yellow drawing pin out of the ball of his foot. He held it up against the light between his thumb and forefinger and showed it to the other customers.

Feldmayer's brain released so many endorphins at the sight of the drawing pin being removed that it almost undid him. Pure joy flooded him for hours on end. Every inhibition and every sense of impotence disappeared at a stroke. He longed to embrace the wounded boy and the entire universe. In the wake of this high, he finally, after many months, managed to sleep through the night and had a recurring dream: the boy pulled out the thorn, stood up, laughed, and waved at him.

A mere ten days went by before the boy with the thorn held out his wounded foot to him again in reproach. Feldmayer groaned, but he knew what had to be done; the little box with the drawing pins was still in his pocket.

He had worked for the museum for twenty-three years and now within a few minutes his time there would be over. Feldmayer stood up and gave his legs a shake; recently they had often gone numb from his sitting so long. Another two minutes, and that would be that. He set the chair under the middle window, the way he had found it on his first day, then straightened it and dusted it with his jacket sleeve, then for the last time he went over to the statue.

He had never in twenty-three years touched the boy pulling out the thorn. Nor had he planned any of what happened next. He saw himself grip the statue with both hands; he felt the smooth, cool marble as he lifted it off the plinth. It was heavier than he expected. He held it up to his face—it was very close to him now—then higher and higher above his head, and then he stood on tiptoes so that it was as high as he could manage. He held it this way for almost a minute, until he began to tremble. He breathed as deeply as he could, then hurled the statue to the floor with all his strength and screamed. Feldmayer screamed louder than he had ever screamed in his whole life. His scream rang through the rooms, bouncing from wall to wall, and was so terrible that a waitress in the museum café nine rooms away dropped a loaded tray. The sculpture shattered on the floor with a dull crash and one of the marble slabs cracked.

Then something strange happened. It seemed to Feldmayer that the blood in his veins changed colour, it turned bright red. He felt it surge and pulse from his stomach, spreading throughout his body, all the way to the tips of his fingers and toes, illuminating him from inside. The cracked marble slab, the indentations in the brick walls, the motes of dust all became three-dimensional. Everything swelled toward him. The flying splinters of marble seemed to stand still in midair. Then he saw the thorn. It glinted with a strange light; he saw it from all sides at once before it dissolved and vanished.

Feldmayer sank to his knees, lifted his head slowly, and looked out of the window. The chestnut tree stood veiled in the soft green that only the first days of spring could summon, and the afternoon sun was casting flickering shadows on the floor of the hall. The pain had ceased. Feldmayer sensed the warmth on his face, his nose itched, and then he began to laugh. He laughed and laughed. He was clutching his stomach with laughter and couldn't stop.

The two policemen who took Feldmayer home were surprised by the meagre furnishings in his apartment. They sat him down on one of the two chairs in the kitchen, intending to wait until he'd calmed down and perhaps would be able to explain things.

One of the policemen went in search of the bathroom. He opened the bedroom door by mistake, stepped into the dark room, and groped for a light switch. And this was when he saw it: the walls and ceiling were papered with thousands of photos, stuck one over the other; there wasn't an empty inch of space. They were even lying on the floor and the night table. Every one of them featured the same thing; only the location changed. Men, women and children sat on steps, on chairs, on sofas, and on window seats; they sat in swimming pools, shoe shops, meadows, and on the banks of lakes. And all of them were pulling a yellow drawing pin out of one foot.

The directors of the museum pressed charges against Feldmayer for damaging their property and wanted to sue him for financial restitution. The prosecutor's office investigated hundreds of cases of grievous bodily harm. The head of the relevant department decided to have Feldmayer examined by an expert psychiatrist. It was a remarkable report. The psychiatrist couldn't make up his mind: on the one hand, he thought Feldmayer had been in the grip of a psychosis; on the other hand, it was possible that he had healed himself by the very act of destroying the statue. Perhaps Feldmayer was dangerous, and one day the drawing pins would be knives instead. But then again, perhaps not.

Finally, the prosecutor brought charges that would involve a trial by jury. This signified that he was going for a sentence of two to four years. When such charges are brought, the judge must decide whether they are sufficient to order a trial. The judge institutes proceedings if he considers that a verdict of guilty is more likely than one of not guilty. At least that's what it says in the textbooks. In reality, quite different questions come into play. No judge likes to have his decision taken up by a higher court, which is why many proceedings are set in motion even though the judge actually thinks he's going to exonerate the accused. If the judge doesn't want to institute proceedings, he sometimes contacts the prosecutor's office to establish that there isn't going to be an appeal.

The judge, the prosecutor and I sat in the judge's office and discussed the case. The prosecution's evidence struck me as sketchy. There were only the photos. No witnesses were cited in the charge. And it was unclear how old the pictures were—the events could have taken place years ago and thus be subject to the statute of limitations. The expert psychiatrist's report didn't provide much support, and Feldmayer had not made any confession. What was left was the damage to the statue. It seemed clear to me that the museum's management bore most of the blame. They had locked Feldmayer in a room for twenty-three years and forgotten him.

The judge agreed with me. He was indignant. He said he

would prefer to see the museum's management sitting where the accused sat; after all, it was the town's administrators who had destroyed a man. The judge wanted the charge revised to reflect a more minor offence. He was extremely explicit. But dropping the graver charges would require the agreement of the prosecution, and our prosecutor wasn't ready to make that agreement.

A few days later, however, I received notification of the reduction in the charges. When I called the judge, he told me our prosecutor's boss had, surprisingly, agreed. The reason was, naturally, never made official, but it was clear nonetheless: if the trial had gone ahead, the museum's management would have been subjected to rather unpleasant questions in open court. And an indignant judge would have given the defence a very free hand. Feldmayer would have come out with a trivial sentence, but the town and the museum would have been made to look very bad.

The museum also eventually gave up on its civil suit. When we had lunch, the director said he was just glad that Feldmayer hadn't been guarding a room with a Salome painting in it.

Feldmayer kept his pension rights. The museum made an almost invisible announcement that a statue had been accidentally damaged; Feldmayer's name was not mentioned, and he never picked up a yellow drawing pin again.

The shards of the statue were collected in a cardboard box and taken to the museum's workshop. A restorer was given the task of putting it back together again. She spread all the pieces out on a table that was covered in black cloth. She photographed every single splinter and entered confirmation on more than two hundred individual pieces in a notebook.

It was silent in the workshop when she began. She had opened a window; the spring warmth suffused the room as she examined the shards and smoked a cigarette. She was happy to be able to work here after finishing her studies. *The Thorn Puller* was her first big job. She knew that putting it back together could last a long time, maybe even years.

A little wooden head of a Buddha from Kyoto stood opposite the table. It was ancient and had a crack in the forehead. The Buddha was smiling.

Love

She had dozed off, her head lying on his thigh. It was a warm summer afternoon, the windows stood open, and she felt good. They had known each other for two years, both of them were studying economics in Bonn, and they attended the same lectures. She knew he was in love with her.

Patrick stroked her back. The book was boring him; he didn't like Hesse, and he was only reading the poems out loud because that's what she wanted. He looked at her naked skin, her spine and shoulder blades, running his fingers over them. The Swiss army knife he'd used to cut the apple they'd eaten was lying on the night table. He laid the book aside and picked up the knife. Her eyes half-closed, she watched as he got an erection. She had to laugh—they'd only just had sex. He opened the blade. She lifted her head toward his penis. Then she felt the cut in her back. She screamed, struck his hand away to one side, and leapt to her feet. The knife flew onto the polished hardwood floor. She felt the blood running down her back. He looked at her, bewildered; she slapped him, seized her clothes from the chair, and ran into the bathroom. His student apartment was on the ground floor of an old building. She dressed hurriedly, climbed out of the window, and ran.

Four weeks later, the police sent the summons to his registered address. And because, like many students, he hadn't given any formal notification of his change of address, the letter didn't land in Bonn, but in his parents' mailbox in Berlin. His mother opened it, thinking it was a ticket of some kind. That evening, the parents first had a long discussion of what they might have done wrong; then the father called Patrick. The next day, his mother made an appointment with my secretary, and a week later the family was sitting in my office.

They were orderly people, the father was a construction foreman, thickset, chinless, short arms and legs, the mother around forty, former secretary, imperious and full of energy. Patrick didn't seem to go with his parents. He was an uncommonly pretty boy, with delicate hands and dark brown eyes. He described the details of the incident. He and Nicole had been together for two years, and they'd never had a fight. His mother interrupted him every second sentence. Then *she* said of course it had been an accident. Patrick said he was sorry. He loved the girl and wanted to apologise to her, but he couldn't reach her anymore.

His mother got a little too loud. 'It's better that way. I don't want you to see her again. Besides which, you're leaving next year anyway to go to the university in St Gallen.'

The father said very little. At the end of the meeting, he asked if things were going to get bad for Patrick.

I thought it was a minor case that would resolve itself quickly. It had already been referred by the police to the prosecutor's office. I called the senior prosecutor, who was preparing the formal examination. She had a wide range of oversight, all so-called DV cases—which is to say domestic violence. There were thousands of such cases every year, caused overwhelmingly by alcohol, jealousy and rows over children. She agreed quickly to let me see the files.

Two days later, I received the contents, barely forty pages, on my computer. The photo of the girl's back showed a six-inch cut with smooth edges to the wound. It would have healed cleanly and left no permanent scar. But I was sure that the cut itself was no accident. A falling knife makes a different kind of wound.

I asked the family to come back for a second discussion, and because the matter wasn't urgent, the appointment was made for three weeks hence.

Five days later, when I locked the office one Thursday evening and switched on the light in the stairwell, Patrick was sitting there on the steps. I asked him to come in, but he shook his head. His eyes were glassy and he was holding an unlit cigarette in his fingers. I went back into the office, collected an ashtray, and offered him a lighter. Then I sat down next to him. The time switch for the light clicked off; we sat in the dark and smoked.

'Patrick, what can I do for you?' I asked after a while.

'It's hard,' he said.

'It's always hard,' I said, and waited.

'I haven't ever told anyone.'

'Take your time; it's quite comfortable here.' In fact, it was cold and it was uncomfortable.

'I love Nicole the way I've never loved anyone, ever. She doesn't call, I've tried everything. I even wrote her a letter, but she never answered. Her mobile phone is switched off. Her best friend hung up when I called.'

'It happens.'

'What do I do?'

'The charge isn't an insoluble problem. You're not going to go to jail. I've read your file…'

'Yes?'

'Honestly, your story doesn't add up. It wasn't an accident.'

Patrick hesitated and lit another cigarette. 'Yes, you're right,' he said; 'it really wasn't an accident. I don't know if I can tell you what really happened.'

'Lawyers are bound by confidentiality,' I said. 'Everything you say to me will remain between us. Only you can decide whether I am allowed to speak, and if so, with whom. Not even your parents will hear anything about this conversation.'

'Is it the same with the police?'

'Most of all with the police and all the other people involved in the prosecution. I have to be silent; if I weren't, I'd make myself legally liable.'

'I still can't talk about it,' he said.

Suddenly, I had an idea. 'There's a lawyer in my office with a five-year-old daughter. Just the other day she told another child something while the two of them were squatting on the floor. She's a very active child, and she talked and talked and talked while she kept sliding over closer to her friend. She was so excited by her own story that she was soon sitting almost right on top of the other girl. She kept on chattering, until finally she couldn't contain herself any longer. She flung her arms around her friend and was so happy and excited, she bit her on the neck.'

I could feel something at work in Patrick. He was struggling with himself. Finally, he said, 'I wanted to eat her.'

'Your girlfriend?'

'Yes.'

'Why did you want to do that?'

'You don't know her; you'd have to have seen her back. Her shoulder blades come together in points; her skin is firm and clear. My skin is full of pores, almost like holes, but hers is dense and smooth, and it has these tiny little blonde hairs on it.'

I tried to recall the picture of her back that was in the file. 'Was it the first time you wanted to?' I asked.

'Yes. Well, only once before, but it wasn't so strong that time. We were on holiday in Thailand; it was when we were lying on the beach. I bit her a little too hard.'

'How did you want to do it this time?'

'I don't know. I think I just wanted to cut out a little slice.'

'Have you ever wanted to eat anyone else?'

'No, of course not. It's all about her, only her.' He dragged on his cigarette. 'Am I crazy? I'm not some Hannibal Lecter. Or am I?' He was afraid of himself.

'No, you're not. I'm not a doctor, but I think you've become too caught up in your love for her. You know that, too, Patrick; you say so yourself. I think you're quite ill. You need to let people help you. And you need to do it soon.'

There are different kinds of cannibalism. People eat people out of hunger, out of obedience to some ritual, or out of severe personality disorders that often take a sexual form. Patrick thought Hollywood had invented Hannibal Lecter, but he's always existed. In Styria in the eighteenth century, Paul Reisiger ate 'the beating hearts of six virgins'—he believed that if he ate nine, he could become invisible. Peter Kürten drank the blood of his victims; in the 1970s, Joachim Kroll ate at least eight people he'd killed; and in 1948, Bernhard Oehme consumed his own sister.

Legal history abounds with the unimaginable. When Karl Denke was captured in 1924, his kitchen was full of human remains of all kinds: pieces of flesh preserved in vinegar, a tubful of bones, pots of rendered fat, and a sack with hundreds of human teeth. He wore suspenders cut from strips of human skin on which nipples were still identifiable. The number of victims remains unknown to this day.

'Patrick, have you ever heard about the Japanese man Issei Sagawa?'

'No, who is he?'

'Sagawa is a restaurant critic in Tokyo right now.'

'So?'

'In 1981 he ate his girlfriend in Paris. He said he loved her too much.'

'Did he eat all of her?'

'At least several pieces.'

'And'—Patrick's voice shook—'did he say how it was?'

'I don't remember exactly. I think he said she tasted of tuna.'

'Ah …'

'The doctors back then diagnosed a severe psychotic disturbance.'

'Is that what I have, too?'

'I don't know exactly, but I want you to go to a doctor.' I switched on the light. 'Please wait here. I'm going to get you the phone number of the emergency psychiatric services. If you want, I'll drive you there now.'

'No,' he said, 'I'd like to think about it first.'

'I can't make you, Patrick. But please come back here to the office first thing tomorrow. I'll go with you to a sensible psychiatrist. Okay?'

He hesitated. Then he said he'd come back, and we got to our feet. 'Can I ask you something else?' said Patrick, and went very quiet. 'What happens if I don't go to a psychiatrist?'

'I'm afraid it'll get worse,' I said. I unlocked the door to my office again to find the phone number and put back the ashtray. When I came back out into the stairwell, Patrick had disappeared.

He didn't show up the next day. A week later, I received a letter and a cheque from his mother. She no longer wished me to represent them, and since the letter was also signed by Patrick, it was valid. I called Patrick, but he didn't want to speak to me. Finally, I withdrew from his defence.

Two years later, I was giving a lecture in Zürich. During the break, an elderly criminal lawyer from St Gallen came over to speak to me. He mentioned Patrick's name and asked if he'd been my client, because Patrick had said some such thing.

I asked what had happened. My colleague said, 'Patrick killed a waitress two months ago; until now, nobody's figured out why.'

The Ethiopian

The pale man was sitting right in the middle of the lawn. He had a strangely lopsided face with protruding ears, and his hair was red. His legs stuck out in front of him and his hands were clutching a bundle of banknotes in his lap. The man was staring at a rotting apple lying next to him, watching the ants biting minuscule fragments out of it and carrying them away.

It was shortly after midday on one of those hellishly hot days of high summer in Berlin when no sensible person would willingly set foot out-of-doors at noon. The narrow square had been artificially conjured between the tall buildings by the city planners; their glass and steel construction reflected the sun, and the heat hovered in a trapped layer above the ground. The lawn sprinklers were broken and the grass would be burned by nightfall.

No one paid attention to the man, not even when alarm

sirens started to howl at the bank across the street. The three radio patrol cars that arrived very shortly afterward raced past him. Police ran into the bank, others blocked off the square, and reinforcements poured in.

A woman in a suit came out of the bank with several policemen. Putting a hand over her brow to protect herself from the sun, she searched the lawn with her eyes and finally pointed to the pale man. A stream of green-and-blue uniforms formed itself immediately in the direction of her outstretched hand. The policemen screamed at the man; one of them drew his service weapon and roared at him to put his hands in the air.

The man didn't react. A police captain, who'd spent the whole day in the precinct house writing up reports and being bored, ran at him, wanting to be the first. He threw himself at the man and yanked his right arm up behind his back. Banknotes flew through the air, orders were yelled, only to be ignored, and then they were all standing around him in a circle, gathering up the money. The man was lying on his stomach while the policeman drilled his knee into his back and pressed his face into the grass. The earth was warm. Looking between all the boots, the man could see the apple again. The ants, unimpressed, were keeping right on with their work. He breathed in the smell of the grass, the earth, and the rotting apple, closed his eyes, and was in Ethiopia again.

His life began the way lives begin in a terrible fairy tale. He was abandoned. A luminously green plastic tub stood on the steps of a vicarage near Giessen. The newborn was lying on a matted coverlet and was suffering from hypothermia. Whoever had put him down there had left him with nothing—no letter, no picture, no memory. That kind of tub was sold in every supermarket; the coverlet was army issue.

The vicar immediately notified the police, but the mother was never found. The baby was taken to an orphanage, and after three months the authorities put him up for adoption. The Michalkas, who had no children of their own, took him in and baptised him with the name of Frank Xaver. They were taciturn, hard people, hop growers from a quiet region of Upper Franconia; they had no experience with children. His adoptive father would say, 'Life isn't a bowl of cherries,' and then stick out his bluish tongue and lick his lips. He handled human stock, livestock and hop-root stock with equal respect and equal strictness. He got angry with his wife when she was too soft with the child. 'You're spoiling him for me,' he said, thinking of shepherds, who never stroke their dogs.

The boy was teased in kindergarten; he started school when he was six. Nothing went well for him. He was ugly, he was too tall and, above all, he was too rebellious. School was hard for him. His spelling was a catastrophe, and he got the lowest marks in almost every class. The girls were frightened of him, or repelled by the way he looked. He was insecure, which made him a loudmouth. His hair made him an outsider. Most people thought he was stupid; only his German teacher said he had other gifts. She sometimes had him make small repairs around the house, and she gave him his first pocketknife. Michalka carved her a wooden windmill for Christmas. The sails turned when you blew on them. The teacher married a man from Nürnberg and left the village during the summer holiday. She hadn't told the boy, and the next time he went to see her, he found the windmill in front of the house in a skip.

Michalka had to repeat a year of classes twice. When high school was over, he left and became an apprentice to a carpenter in the next-biggest town. No one teased him anymore; he was almost six foot six. He passed his qualifying exam to become an apprentice only because he was outstanding in the practical section. He did his military service in a unit of the signal corps near Nürnberg. He picked a fight with his superiors and spent a day in the brig.

After his discharge, he hitchhiked to Hamburg. He'd seen a film that took place in the city. It had beautiful women, broad streets, a port, and real nightlife. Everything had to be better there. 'Freedom lives in Hamburg,' he'd read somewhere.

The owner of a construction carpentry firm in Fuhlsbüettel took him on and gave him a room at the top of the factory building. The room was clean. Michalka was skilled and they were pleased with him. Although he often didn't know the technical terms, he understood the technical drawings, corrected them, and could implement them. When money was stolen from a locker, the firm dismissed him. He was the last person to have been hired, and there had never been a theft at the company before. The police found the cash box in the apartment of a drug addict two weeks later— Michalka had had nothing to do with it.

On the Reeperbahn, he ran into an old buddy from the

army, who got him a job as janitor in a brothel. Michalka became the gofer. He got to know those on the margins of society—pimps, moneylenders, prostitutes, addicts, thugs. He kept himself out of it as best he could. He lived for two years in a dark room in the basement of the brothel, and then he began to drink, unable to bear the misery that surrounded him. The girls in the brothel liked him and told him their stories. He couldn't cope. He got into debt with the wrong people. He couldn't pay them back, and so the interest kept rising. He was beaten up, left lying in a doorway, and then picked up by the police. Michalka knew that any more of this would be the death of him.

He decided to try things abroad; he didn't care which country he landed in. He didn't spend a lot of time thinking it over. He took a stocking from one of the girls in the brothel. Entering the savings bank, he stretched it over his face, the way he'd seen it done in a movie, threatened the cashier with a plastic pistol, and made off with twelve thousand deutschmarks. The police blocked off the streets and checked everyone who was on foot, but Michalka, in a kind of trance, had gotten on a bus headed to the airport. He bought an economy ticket to Addis Ababa because he thought the city was in Asia, or at least far away. Nobody stopped him. Four hours after the holdup he was sitting in the plane, his only luggage a plastic bag. When the plane took off, he was afraid.

After a ten-hour flight, the first plane trip in his life, he landed in the capital of Ethiopia. He bought a visa for six months at the airport.

Five million inhabitants, sixty thousand children on the streets, prostitution, petty crime, poverty, innumerable beggars, cripples by the sides of the roads showing off their deformities to arouse pity—after three weeks, Michalka knew that there was nothing to choose between the misery in Hamburg and the misery in Addis Ababa. He came across a few Germans, a colony of human wrecks. The state of hygiene was catastrophic. Michalka came down with typhus. He ran a fever, his skin broke out in a rash, and he had dysentery, until finally an acquaintance found a doctor, who gave him antibiotics. Once again, he'd reached the end.

Michalka was now convinced that the world was a rubbish dump. He had no friends, no prospects, nothing that could hold him. After six months in Addis Ababa, he decided to end his life, suicide as a form of reckoning. But he didn't want to die in the dirt. There were still about five thousand marks of the money left over. He took the train toward Djibouti. A few kilometres beyond Dire Dawa, he began his wanderings through the pastureland. He slept on the ground or in tiny cheap hostels; he was bitten by a mosquito, which infected him with malaria. He took a bus up into the highlands. The malaria broke out along the way and he started to shake. He got out at some point, sick and confused, and lost his way in the coffee plantations as the world swam in a haze before his eyes. He stumbled and fell to the ground between the rows of coffee bushes. Before he lost consciousness, his last thought was, It was all such shit.

Between two bouts of fever, Michalka woke up. He realised that he was in a bed, and a doctor and a lot of strange people were gathered around him. They were all black. He understood that the people were helping him, and he sank back into his fevered nightmares. The malaria was brutal. Here in the highlands, there were no mosquitoes, but people were familiar with the illness and knew how to treat it. The peculiar stranger they'd found in the plantation would survive.

The fever slowly ebbed, and Michalka slept for almost twenty-four hours. When he awoke, he was lying alone in a whitewashed room. His jacket and trousers had been washed and arranged neatly on the only stool in the room, and his rucksack was standing next to it. When he tried to get up, his legs buckled and everything turned black before his eyes. He sat on the bed and stayed like that for fifteen minutes. Then he tried again. He desperately needed to go to the toilet. He opened the door and stepped out into the hall. A woman came at him, gesticulating wildly and shaking her head: no, no, no. She linked her arm into his and forced him back into the room. He made his need clear to her. She nodded and pointed to a bucket under the bed. He found her beautiful, and went back to sleep.

When he woke up next time, he felt better. He looked in his rucksack; all the money was still there. He could leave the room. He was alone in the tiny house, which consisted of two rooms and a kitchen. Everything was clean and orderly. He went out of the house and into a little village square. The air was fresh and pleasantly cool. Children came storming up to him, laughing and wanting to take hold of his red hair. Once he understood this, he sat down on a stone and let them do it. The children had their fun. Then at some point, the beautiful woman in whose house he was staying arrived. She scolded and pulled at him, got him back inside the house, and gave him corn cakes. He ate them all. She smiled at him.

Slowly, he got to know the coffee farmers' village. They had found him in the plantation, carried him up the hill, and fetched a doctor from the town. They were friendly to him. After he'd regained his strength, he wanted to help. The farmers were astonished; then they accepted.

Six months later, he was still living with the woman, slowly learning her language. First her name: Ayana. He wrote words down phonetically in a notebook. They laughed when he pronounced things wrong. Sometimes she ran her fingers through his red hair. At some point, they kissed. Ayana was twenty-one. Her husband had died two years before in an accident in the provincial capital.

Michalka thought about coffee growing. The harvest was laborious; it was performed by hand between October and March. He quickly grasped the problem: the village was the last link in the chain of trade. The man who collected the dried coffee beans earned more and had less work. But the man owned an old truck, and nobody in the village knew how to drive. For fourteen hundred dollars Michalka bought a better vehicle and drove the crop to the factory himself. He obtained nine times the price and divided the earnings among the farmers. Then he taught Dereje, one of the young men in the village, how to drive. Dereje and he now collected beans from the neighbouring villages as well, and paid the farmers three times what they'd been getting before. Soon they were able to buy a second truck.

Michalka wondered how it might be possible to make the work easier. He drove to the provincial capital, acquired an ancient diesel generator, and used old wheel rims and steel cables to build a cable rail from the plantation to the village. For containers he carpentered together big wooden chests. The rail broke down twice before he worked out the right distance between the wooden supporting beams and rein-forced them with steel braces. The village elder observed his experiments with suspicion, but when the cable railway started to run properly, he was the first to clap Michalka on the back. The coffee beans could now be transported faster, and the farmers no longer had to haul them to the village on their backs. They could harvest more quickly and the work was less exhausting. The children loved the cable railway, they painted the wooden chests with faces and animals and a man with red hair.

Michalka wanted to keep improving the yield. The farmers spread the beans out on racks and turned them for five weeks, until they were almost dry. The racks stood outside the huts or on their roofs. The beans spoiled if they got wet and the spread layers had to be thin to prevent rot from setting in. It was demanding work, which each farmer had to do for himself. Michalka bought cement and mixed concrete. He made a flat surface at the edge of the village, which could be used by all the farmers for their crops. He constructed large rakes, and now the farmers could turn the beans together. They stretched clear sheets of plastic above the platform to keep off the rain, and the beans under it dried quicker. The farmers were happy. It was less work and nothing rotted anymore.

Michalka realised the quality of the coffee could be improved if the beans weren't just dried. The village lay close to a small river that ran clear from its source. He washed fresh-picked coffee beans by hand and sorted them into three water tanks. With a little money, he hired a dealer to buy a machine that separated the flesh of the fruit from the beans. The first experiments went wrong; the beans thus stripped of the fruit pulp fermented too long and went bad. He learned it was a matter of keeping the equipment absolutely clean; even a single leftover bean could spoil the whole process. Finally, it worked. He washed the coffee that had been prepared with fresh water and got rid of the remains of the parchment-like skin of the beans. He bordered off a little area on the concrete slab and dried them. When he took a sack of these beans to the dealer, he received three times the usual price. Michalka explained the process to the farmers; using the cable railway, they could bring in the harvest so quickly that the beans would be going through their water bath within twelve hours. After two years, the village was producing the best coffee beans for miles around.

Ayana became pregnant. They rejoiced about the child. When the little girl was born, they named her Tiru. Michalka was proud and happy. He knew he owed his life to Ayana.

The village became prosperous. After three years, there were five trucks, the harvest was perfectly organised, the farmers' plantations were growing larger, and they had installed a watering system and planted trees to form a windbreak. Michalka was respected and known throughout the neighbourhood. The farmers placed a portion of their earnings into a communal cash box. Michalka had brought a young teacher from the town to make sure that the village children learned to read and write.

If someone in the village fell ill, Michalka took care of them. The doctor had put together a kit of emergency supplies and taught him the rudiments of medical knowledge. He learned quickly; he saw how septicemia was handled, and assisted at births. In the evenings, the doctor often sat with Michalka and Ayana, telling them the long history of the Holy Land. They became friends.

When quarrels broke out, it was the man with the red hair who was asked for advice. Michalka would not allow himself to be bribed, and he judged the way a good judge does, without regard to clan or village. People trusted him.

He had found his life. Ayana and he loved each other; Tiru was growing and was healthy. Michalka couldn't grasp his good fortune. Only sometimes, but less and less often, did the nightmares return. When that happened, Ayana would wake up and stroke him. She said her language had no word for the past. The years with her made Michalka soft-tempered and calm.

At some point, Michalka attracted the attention of the authorities. They wanted to see his passport. His visa had long since expired; he'd been living in Ethiopia for six years now. They were polite but insisted that he go to the capital to clarify matters. Michalka had a bad feeling as he said good-bye. Dereje took him to the airport. His family waved after him; Ayana wept.

In Addis Ababa, he was sent to the German embassy.

An official checked the computer and disappeared with his passport. Michalka had to wait for an hour. When the official appeared again, he looked grim, and two guards were accompanying him. Michalka was taken into custody and the official read him the arrest order of a judge in Hamburg. Bank robbery. The damning evidence, the fingerprints he'd left on the counter in the bank. His fingerprints were on file because he'd once been involved in a fight. Michalka tried to pull himself free. He was pushed down onto the floor and handcuffed. After a night in the cell in the basement of the embassy, he was flown to Hamburg in the company of two security guards and led before the examining magistrate. Three months later, he was sentenced to a minimum of five years. The sentence was mild, because it had all happened a long time ago and Michalka had no previous convictions.

He couldn't write to Ayana because there wasn't even an official address. The German embassy in Addis Ababa couldn't, or wouldn't, help him. And of course there was no phone in the village. He had no photo. He barely uttered a word, and became solitary. Day stretched after day, month after month, year after year.

After three years, for the first time he was granted privileges and unaccompanied daytime release. He wanted to go home immediately; he couldn't go back to prison. But he had neither the money for the flight nor a passport. He knew where he could get both. In jail, he'd picked up the address of a forger in Berlin. So that's where he hitchhiked. In the meantime, they were searching for him. He found the forger, but the forger wanted to see some money. Michalka had almost none.

He was in despair. He wandered the streets for three days without eating or drinking. He struggled with himself. He didn't want to commit a new crime, but he had to get home to his family, to Ayana and Tiru.

Eventually, he used the last of his prison money to buy a toy pistol at the train station and went into the first bank he saw. He looked at the cashier as he held the pistol with the barrel pointed down. His mouth was dry. He said very quietly, 'I need money. Please excuse me. I really need it.' At first, she didn't understand him; then she gave him the money. Later, she said she'd 'sympathised'. She took the money from the pile that had been specially prepared for such attacks and thus triggered the silent alarm. He took it, laid the pistol on the counter, and said, 'I'm so sorry. Please forgive me.' There was a stretch of green grass outside the bank. He couldn't run away anymore. He walked really slowly, then sat down and simply waited. Michalka had come to the end for the third time.

One of Michalka's cell mates asked me to take on the case. He knew Michalka from Hamburg and said he'd pay for the defence. I visited Michalka in the prison in Moabit. He handed me the warrant on the regular red paper used by the court: bank robbery, plus the remaining twenty months from the old sentence in Hamburg. Any defence seemed pointless, Michalka had been captured in the act, and he had already been convicted of the same crime before. So the only question was going to be the length of the sentence, and that, naturally, was going to be dreadfully long. But something about Michalka impressed me; there was something different about him. The man was not a typical bank robber. I took on his defence.

In the weeks that followed, I often visited Michalka. At the beginning, he barely spoke to me. He seemed to have finished with life. Very gradually, he opened up a little and began to tell me his story. He didn't want to divulge anything; he believed he'd be betraying his wife and daughter if he spoke their names in jail.

The defence can demand that a defendant be examined by a psychiatrist or psychologist. The court will accede to such a demand if it is likely to succeed in bringing out facts that suggest the defendant suffers from some form of mental illness, a disorder, or a striking behavioural peculiarity. Of course, the expert's report is not binding on the court—the psychiatrist cannot *decide* if the accused is not criminally responsible or has diminished responsibility. Only the court can decide these matters. But the expert who writes the report helps the court by giving the judges the scientific fundamentals.

It was obvious that Michalka was disturbed at the time of the crime. Nobody apologises in the course of a bank robbery, sits down in a meadow with the stolen cash, and waits to be arrested. The court ordered a psychiatric evaluation, and two months later the written report appeared. The psychiatrist was proceeding from a conclusion of diminished capacity. He would go into all other details at the trial.

The trial opened five months after Michalka's arrest. The court was conducted by a presiding judge, plus her junior, and two female jurors. The presiding judge had set aside a mere day for the proceedings. Michalka admitted he had committed the bank robbery. He spoke hesitatingly and too softly. The police reported how they had arrested Michalka. They described how he had been sitting on the grass. The police captain who'd nailed him said Michalka had put up no resistance.

The cashier said she hadn't felt at all afraid. She had felt sorry for the robber more than anything, as he'd looked so sad. 'Like a dog,' she said. The prosecutor asked if she now experienced anxiety at work, if she'd had to report in sick or had to undergo any course of therapy for the victims of crimes. She said no to all of it. The robber had just been a poor soul, and more polite than most of their customers. The prosecutor was obliged to ask these questions: if the witness really had been afraid, it would have been grounds for a higher sentence.

The toy pistol was introduced into evidence. It was a cheap model from China, weighing only a few grams and looking utterly harmless. When one of the jurors picked it up, it slipped, fell to the floor, and a piece of plastic broke off. It was impossible to take such a weapon seriously.

After the crime itself has been laid out during a trial, it is customary for the accused to be questioned about his 'personal circumstances'.

Michalka was almost entirely withdrawn the whole time; it was hard to move him, at least initially, to tell the story of his life. It was only slowly, piece by piece, that he could try to recount it. He barely succeeded; words failed him. Like many people, he found it hard to express his feelings. It seemed simpler to let the expert psychiatrist present the life of the accused.

The psychiatrist was well prepared and he laid out Michalka's life in every detail. The judge knew all this already from the written report, but it was new information for the jurors. They were paying attention. The psychiatrist had questioned Michalka over an unusually long series of sessions. When he finished, the presiding judge turned to Michalka to ask if the expert had rendered it all accurately. Michalka nodded and said, 'Yes, he did.'

Then the expert witness was questioned about his professional evaluation of the accused's psychic state during the bank robbery. The psychiatrist explained that the three days Michalka had spent wandering around the city without food or drink had measurably diminished his capacity for rational behaviour. Michalka had hardly known what he was doing anymore, and he had lost almost all control over his actions. The hearing of evidence was concluded.

During a recess in the trial, Michalka said none of it had any point; no matter how much trouble people were going to, he was going to be found guilty anyway.

In a trial, it is the prosecutor who presents his closing argument first. Unlike in the United States or England, the prosecutor takes no position; he or she is neutral. The prosecutor's office is neutral; it also establishes exonerating circumstances, and thus it neither wins nor loses—the only passion in the prosecutor's office is for the law. The law is all it serves—that, and justice. That at least is the theory.

And during preliminary proceedings, it is the rule. But circumstances often change in the heat of a trial, and objectivity begins to suffer in the process. That is only human, because a good prosecutor is always a prosecutor, and it is more than difficult both to prosecute and to remain neutral. Perhaps it is a flaw woven into the very fabric of our criminal justice system; perhaps the law simply demands too much.

The prosecutor demanded nine years for Michalka. He said he didn't believe Michalka's story. It was 'too fantastic and probably a total invention'. Nor did he want to accept an argument of diminished capacity, because the psychiatrist's explanations rested solely on the accused's statements and lacked substantiation. The only fact was that Michalka had committed a bank robbery. 'The minimum sentence for bank robbery in the law is five years,' he said. 'It is the second time the defendant has committed this offence. The only admissible cause for leniency is that the money was secured and he made a full confession. Nine years are thus the appropriate sentence for the crime and the defendant's guilt.'

Of course it cannot all turn on whether a defendant's statements are *believed*. In court, what is at issue is proof. The accused thus has an advantage: he doesn't have to prove anything, neither his innocence nor the accuracy of his statement. But there are different rules for the prosecutor's office and the court: they may not state anything that they cannot prove. This sounds much simpler than it is. No one is so objective as to be able always to distinguish conjecture from proof. We believe we know something for sure, we get carried away, and it's often far from simple to find our way back.

Final arguments are no longer decisive in trials these days. The prosecutor's office and the defence are not speaking to sworn witnesses, but to judges and juries. Every false tone, every bit of hair tearing, and every pretentious turn of phrase is unendurable. The great closing arguments belong to earlier centuries. The Germans no longer tolerate pathos; there's been too much of that already.

But sometimes one can allow oneself a little dramatic production, an unanticipated final request. Michalka himself knew nothing about it.

An acquaintance of mine worked in the diplomatic service. She was stationed in Kenya, and she helped me. By many roundabout routes, she had located Michalka's friend, the doctor from the local town. The doctor spoke perfect English. I had talked to him on the phone and begged him to testify as a witness. When I told him I would cover the cost of the airfare, he laughed at me and said he was so happy his friend was still alive that he would go anywhere to see him. And now he was waiting outside the door to the courtroom.

From one moment to the next, Michalka woke up. He leapt to his feet as the doctor entered the court, tears poured down his face, and he tried to get to him. The guards held him captive, but the presiding judge waved them away and allowed it. The two men embraced right in the middle of the courtroom, Michalka lifting the small-boned man right off his feet and hugging him. The doctor had brought a video, and a guard was sent off to get a player. We saw the village, the cable railway, the trucks, all the children and grown-ups, who kept laughing into the camera and calling 'Frroank, Frroank.' And then at last we saw Ayana and Tiru. Michalka wept and laughed and wept again, completely beside himself. He sat next to his friend and almost squashed the doctor's fingers in his own enormous hands. The presiding judge and one of the witnesses had tears in their eyes. It was nothing like a normal scene in a courtroom.

Our system of criminal law is based on the requirement of personal guilt. We punish according to someone's guilt; we ask to what extent we can make him responsible for his actions. It's complicated. In the Middle Ages, things were simpler: punishment was only commensurate with the act itself. A thief had his hand chopped off. It was all the same, no matter whether he'd stolen out of greed or because he would otherwise have starved. Punishment in those days was a form of mathematics; every act carried a precisely established weight of retribution. Our contemporary criminal law is more intelligent, it is more just as regards life, but it is also more difficult. A bank robbery really isn't always just a bank robbery. What could we accuse Michalka of? Had he not done what all of us are capable of? Would we have behaved differently if we had found ourselves in his place? Is it not everyone's deepest desire to return to those they love?

Michalka was sentenced to two years. A week after the trial, I ran into the presiding judge in one of the long halls in the court building in Moabit. She said the jurors were getting together to buy him an air ticket.

After Michalka had served half his sentence, he was released on probation. The presiding judge at the parole hearing, a wise old man, had them run through the whole story all over again, and just muttered 'wild'. Then he ordered Michalka set free.

Michalka is back living in Ethiopia today and has acquired full citizenship. Tiru now has a brother and a sister. Sometimes Michalka calls me. He still tells me that he's happy.

Ceci n'est pas une pomme.